And Then There Were Scones

The Parchment Paper Mysteries, Volume 1

Matilda Swift

Published by Matilda Swift, 2025.

This is a work of fiction. Similarities to real people, places, or events are entirely coincidental.

AND THEN THERE WERE SCONES

First edition. February 12, 2025.

Copyright © 2025 Matilda Swift.

Written by Matilda Swift.

By Matilda Swift

The Heathervale Mysteries
Rotten to the Marrow (prequel novella)
The Slay of the Land
Dying over Spilled Milk
Fresh out of Cluck
The Scream of the Crop
A Room with a Clue
Wreathed in Mystery (short story collection)
The Slippery Spoon Mysteries
Take the Rough with the Smoothie (prequel novella)
From Bad to Wurst
In Deep Truffle
Butter Late than Never
The Parchment Paper Mysteries
Artichoke Heart of Darkness (prequel novella)
And Then There Were Scones
Lime and Punishment
For Whom the Bell Pepper Tolls
The Catcher in the Pie

Dedication and Notes

For Miss Marple and Madame Poirot, the purr-fect writing companions.

***

What wild desires, what restless torments seize
The hapless man, who feels the book-disease...
John Ferriar

***

Note: This book is written in British English. In Little Quillington, people eat biscuits rather than cookies, wear trousers rather than pants, say "got" instead of "gotten," and use all manner of charming spellings that should help you feel more at home in this book's cosy English setting.

***

Get Matilda Swift's starter library for free by signing up to her newsletter. Grab exclusive bonus content, including free books, and issue 1 of Little Quillington's local paper, *The Quill*, at the end of *And Then There Were Scones*. But first, curl up with plenty of murders, mysteries, and mugs of tea.

1

"Please tell me you have some butter," Jessica Askew called as she raced across the hardwood floor of her best friend's shop. She slammed into the high walnut counter, rattling the keys of its antique brass till. Ginger curls sprang from her ponytail, and Jessica raked them sharply from her face.

"Some what?" The muffled voice coming from the storeroom didn't carry even a hint of urgency. But Jessica knew better than to go back there for butter. Even Madame Poirot, the spoiled shop cat, was not permitted near the pin-neat shelving system of Just My Type.

"Butter!" Jessica called, her voice much louder and several notes higher now. Precious seconds were slipping away. She peered forlornly into the shop's enormous and extremely empty fridge. "But I'd settle for a cow, a pail, and a churn." She tapped her left foot, willing energy through her sturdy brown boot and into the shop's sleepy atmosphere.

The shopkeeper, Pippa Pankhurst, finally stepped from the storeroom and propped her hands on her generous hips. "You're a milkmaid now?"

Jessica's heart rose like a soufflé at the sight of her best friend. "I don't shy away from hard work, not in the face of a crisis. I'm on a baking deadline, but I'm missing one key ingredient, and there's not a block of the stuff to be found."

The quaint Yorkshire village of Little Quillington contained all manner of quirky shops, including Pickwick's, the quill-makers'; Novel Scents, where literary settings were recreated in perfumes; and a bookish gift emporium called

Shelf Indulgence. What the village didn't sell anywhere that day was butter.

"What were you expecting on the weekend of the summer fête?" Pippa's thick strawberry-blonde hair swished as she cocked her head. "The scone makers have snapped up every butter block for miles around." Then her mouth dropped open. "Did you forget about the fête?"

"I didn't...forget." Jessica pushed up her soft, willow-green sleeves. "I just perhaps didn't exactly, entirely remember." The summer fête had once been circled on her calendar, and winning the blue ribbon for her scones had been a dream come true. But now she had her eyes on a far bigger baking prize—one she couldn't win without at least one block of butter.

When she'd seen the banners and bunting hung along every street during her arrival in the village that morning, her heart had plummeted straight to her toes. She'd raced into the first shop she passed but found nothing there or in the next one. Pippa's shop, which was on a quiet road off the main square, was her final hope. The shop's confusing name of Just My Type and window display of antique typewriters—which Pippa's father had repaired and sold for years and which she still couldn't part with—often kept food shoppers away.

Jessica had prayed some butter survived the fête preparations here. But this shop's dairy section, too, was empty, and she seriously considered kicking herself for such poor planning. Since she was six feet tall, however, her long legs could cause quite an injury.

"You. Forgot. The fête." A deep dimple punctuated Pippa's lopsided grin. "I suppose it's understandable. I mean, now you're a big TV star, you can't be expected to recall the lives of us little people."

"I'm not a star." Jessica pressed her hands to cheeks as hot as jalapeños, but her clammy fingers did nothing to cool her fierce blush.

Pippa pointed at the newspaper rack by the door, where a row of front covers bore Jessica's face. The shop cat, a dainty tuxedo with snow-white socks and a black heart on one leg, presided over them from her perch among the magazines. Madame Poirot purred loudly.

"Stop collecting these. It's bad enough you send me photos of them." Jessica stacked the papers and shoved them on the counter. They were from several weeks earlier, when she'd first appeared on a televised baking contest and journalists had latched onto her famous last name.

"So, this butter you're looking for," Pippa said slowly, a second dimple appearing on her face, "how valuable is it to you?"

Jessica recognised her best friend's tone. "What do you want for it?"

"Me? Want something? Who says I have butter anyway?"

"Thirty years of friendship says so." Thirty-one, now, Jessica realised. Her latest birthday had passed almost unnoticed in the haze of competition. But what was another year when they'd been friends for a lifetime?

Pippa danced her purple-tipped fingers across the polished shop counter. "Just because you're too big and important for the folks back home, that doesn't mean we've forgotten you."

With a dramatic flourish, she reached under the counter and pulled out a sharp-edged rectangle wrapped in waxed paper.

Butter. Jessica held her breath. The 250-gram block was good but not nearly enough.

Then Pippa took out another block and another—500 grams, 750 grams. "I set these aside the moment you said you were coming." She continued laying blocks on the counter until she'd stacked up a tall pyramid of cool, perfect butter that made Jessica's knees weak. The total was almost four kilograms of butter, which today was more valuable than gold. "Just don't tell Mrs Merdle. She's had to make her scones with margarine, and she'll be sticking pins in an effigy of me as we speak."

"You're a goddess. A miracle worker. An angel in disguise." Jessica opened her favourite Julia Child tote, which said Never Apologise on one side and *Bon Appétit* on the other. But as she reached to slide the butter into the bag, Pippa slapped her hand away.

"Goddesses require tributes."

"Of course," Jessica said with a wry grin. "My new recipe will need extensive taste-testing this evening." She was relieved when Pippa nudged the pyramid of butter closer to her, and Jessica packed it up rapidly. "I expect your criticism to be as blunt as always, so a little liquid courage may be needed. Meet you in the Quill and Well? Drinks are on me."

"I'm closing at eight. I'll meet you then, and I'll be sure to bring an extremely hearty appetite."

Jessica raced through the door onto Verse View, the butter-filled tote banging against her hip, and with her mind already on her recipe. With the missing ingredient secured, she could perfect her next bake for the contest.

Then she turned the corner to the village square and saw who was standing in its centre. Jessica's feet stopped. Her heart sank like a sponge taken out of the oven too soon. This was the last person she wanted to see.

2

Hundreds of people flowed in and out of the shop-lined village square, their smiles as bright as the sun overhead. They milled around, waiting for the parade that would kick off the day's festivities, filling every spare inch with excitement. But nobody crossed the centre of the square. There, a clear ring formed around a familiar black-clad figure.

"'Proud' is not the word I would use in regard to Jessica, no." Those words came from Jessica's aunt Enriqueta, who spoke directly into a camera, her usual sneer sharpened by the tight pull of a bun.

A warm breeze ruffled Jessica's ginger curls, which made her burning cheeks itch. But she couldn't brush her curls away. She couldn't move. It was all she could do to nod at Mr Hoffman's passing wave.

"We loved your strudel muffins last week," the old librarian called. "And everyone says your baked Alaska technical should have taken first place."

He waved once more as his daughters led him through the crowd to a bench. The oldest daughter was guarding the ornately carved seat with half a dozen bags and her fiercest glare—she must have been up since dawn to snag the space. Jessica's heart ached at that kindness and the hugs they wrapped each other in.

Her own family was different from this scenario in every possible way. She turned back to her aunt, whose long black dress and black shoes made her look ready for a wake.

"Our family is proud of Rudyard," the thin-lipped woman continued, "who manages the Houses of Parliament's archives, and proud of his brother Kipling, the authenticator of hieroglyphic scrolls for the British Museum."

Jessica's legs still refused to budge. Her heart pounded against her ribs, as though trying to propel her anywhere else. But she remained squarely in place.

"You must at least be watching Jessica on the show." She couldn't see the face of the man saying this—he stood between a mic operator and a camerawoman, facing Aunt Enriqueta. His jacket was familiar, though. It was the same bright orange Jessica had been surrounded by for weeks, the official colour of *The Great British Street Bakes Showdown*. This mouthful of a TV contest for food truck owners was in its ninth week, and Jessica was through to the semifinal.

She closed her eyes and focused on the contest. Through heat waves that had made ice cream impossible and thunderstorms that were scary enough to curdle milk, she'd succeeded, week after week.

The food-truck business was a tough one, but after leaving Little Quillington, she'd kept her rainbow-sprinkled pink beauty on the road for ten years. All she needed was an extra push to take her to the big leagues. Spots at the UK's major food festivals were impossible to come by, and they were what she needed to make her business a sure and solid success. That was exactly what she'd get by winning this contest.

She was so close to the final she could taste it. Sweet, cinnamon syrup ran in her veins when she pictured herself winning. Now that her closest competitor, Cameron, "the tattooed bad boy of baking," had gone home, she could really do this.

The main hurdle on her way to victory was this home-village visit. The show had made it clear there was no getting out of it—if she wanted to stay in the contest, the production company needed interviews with people from her past and clips of her food truck serving smiling locals. They'd stitch that footage into a segment to make the audience's hearts melt. That was the goal anyway. Jessica didn't think her family would have quite the desired effect.

She opened her eyes just in time to see Aunt Enriqueta answer the orange-jacketed man. *Was she watching Jessica on the show?* The breeze snatched away Aunt Enriqueta's reply, but her thin lips declared a clear and disdainful *no.* The sight burrowed into Jessica's brain, like a crab into sand, ready to scuttle out and nip her when least expected.

Jessica wanted to scuttle away too. She could leave now—head back to her food truck and drive out of the village. She'd have to face Pippa before leaving and see her devastation that she'd quit. But right then, that seemed a far better prospect than reopening old wounds with her family.

The Askews didn't know who she really was, and they didn't want to. They'd made her feel like she was betraying their legacy when—

"Great timing," the orange-jacketed interviewer bellowed, interrupting Jessica's spiralling thoughts and beckoning her over to him.

Everything was "great" in TV-land. A great take, a great segment, a great interview. Such a pronouncement was always followed by a request to do it again but differently.

Jessica's wide smile was automatic. But then she felt the chill of Aunt Enriqueta's attention, and her face fell. Her feet grew roots. She shouldn't have agreed to do this. Coming home for the show had been a mistake.

The church bell rang in the distance. Its single chime, low and resonant, said the time was quarter to twelve. The summer fête's kick-off parade would start in fifteen minutes. Then, the square would swarm with toddlers dressed as bees. These would be followed by a float topped by that year's Sherlock Holmes. The interview in the centre of the square would be swept aside by all this activity.

Jessica closed her eyes once more. She pictured herself winning the baking show. She focused hard on the prize—year-round pitches at the biggest food festivals in the UK. That would mean the end to long application forms and uncertain pitches, an end to pinching pennies so tightly she left fingerprints. The victory would change everything.

Could she stride over and smile on camera with Aunt Enriqueta? Could she do that for just fifteen minutes? That was her timer setting for perfect scones and extra-large oatmeal cookies. The seconds sped by in her kitchen. But would they be as swift with her aunt at her side?

3

"I'm Pablo!" the orange-jacketed man shouted proudly, as though having this name were an achievement, while waving Jessica in like an airplane. "And I know who you are, of course."

With her stiff legs, Jessica sidestepped a gaggle of teens as she reached the middle of the square. She glanced at the loud man's lanyard and saw he was the Outside Broadcast Director, so he was in charge of this new crew sent to capture her hometown.

"Your aunt's helped us get some fantastic B-roll," he said, guiding Jessica like a puppet to stand beside the black-clad woman.

Jessica gave her TV smile once again. She knew exactly what her aunt would have shown them—her own shop, Criminally Good Mysteries, on nearby Askew Avenue.

Pablo rubbed his stubble, looked at the framing, and nudged Jessica closer to her aunt. "Now, we need some face time. Let's get viewers really invested in your story. We want to be up close and personal with our final few contestants."

Jessica took a deep breath and forced herself to widen her smile. "If it's the personal touch you're looking for, there's no better place than my truck. I'd love to show you the latest Rolling Pin upgrades." She pointed in the direction of her rainbow-sprinkled pink food truck. "New gadgets are always a hit, and I can give you the exclusive first look. I've also got a batch of scones that I'm sure your hard-working crew would love." She would, in fact, offer anything to get away from Aunt Enriqueta. Contempt came off her in waves.

"Great idea," Pablo said, circling his finger at the camerawoman to indicate that she should keep rolling. "Just a few questions here first, yeah? Let's start easy. Tell me what Little Quillington means to you."

Jessica tensed at the *harumph* that came from her aunt. But she could still drag up the answer she'd prepared. "It's a beautiful place, and everyone here is so creative." She gestured at the cheerful crowd of brightly dressed people, who were packed into a square lined with quaint, traditional shops, overflowing flowerpots, and neatly clipped topiary. "I get a lot of compliments on the inventiveness of my bakes, and I'm sure this village is where my inspiration comes from."

Aunt Enriqueta stepped closer to the camerawoman. "Little Quillington is a unique jewel in the English landscape. The Askew family founded it over two hundred years ago, and it remains the largest and most significant book village in the nation. Our literary history goes back to famed collector Anthony Askew, and young people in each generation have the immense privilege of inheriting a shop here to—"

"Great stuff," Pablo said, with a look sharp enough to cut steel.

Jessica willed him to ask about Hay-on-Wye, the more famous book town over the border in Wales. Hay-on-Wye was the great thorn in her Aunt Enriqueta's side. She resented the distant relatives who'd set up shops there.

But Pablo had a different focus. He turned to Jessica. "Tell us about your earliest memories of baking. What did you make for your aunt here as a kid?"

Jessica didn't even glance at the woman in black. "My earliest baking memories are with my grandma. She raised me, and she's always loved baking for the family and—"

"She has *always* been dedicated to literature," Aunt Enriqueta interrupted, her voice hard enough to make Jessica step back. "That is the life of an Askew, my mother included. In fact, she is currently travelling to Buckingham Palace at the invitation of the royal family, as part of this lifelong work."

Jessica felt a pang of longing. Her soft, rosemary-scented grandma was as passionate about books as the rest of the family. But she was also overjoyed at Jessica's baking success. She was the only member of the family who'd contacted her about the contest, and she wished her luck before every episode.

"Sounds great," Pablo said. "Can you say more on this royal connection, Jessica? Viewers eat up that sort of thing."

"My grandma's, uh, taking a rare book to the palace. To Buckingham Palace." Jessica felt her skin's protective hardness turning as brittle as spun sugar. She was only comfortable on film, with a mixing bowl in her hand and a bake underway. "It's a gift from the family—from our family, the Askews—to the royal collection." This book donation was the only upside to her grandma being absent that day. The insurance conditions of the delivery meant that her older brother—who would be even worse on camera than Aunt Enriqueta—was accompanying her, along with the village's resident police officer, to keep them safe.

Before Pablo could ask Jessica anything else, a cluster of children dressed as bees gathered around his legs. "Watch it!"

The shock on his face said he'd expected today's parade to consist of a couple of trumpets and some signs painted on bedsheets. But soon, the square would be as lively as an overfilled pan of popcorn over a fierce heat.

Jessica needed to get to her truck and practise her recipe. The baking was going to be filmed and judged the following day, and there were points on the line—points she was desperate to bank now her main competitor, Cameron, was out of the contest. Pretty, young Leah was not far behind. She was popular with viewers, but she struggled with technical challenges. Jessica could almost taste victory, and it was delicious. Despite a near wipe-out from a collapsed sponge early on—which she still couldn't understand; the recipe was foolproof—Jessica was *this close* to success. She could cement her win with one more great bake.

When she turned back to tell Pablo that she really had to go, she found him pressed tightly against an ornate black lamppost, looking as though the surge of toddling bees at his feet threatened to sting him. His artful stubble, tousled hair, and tiny hooped earrings said a village parade wasn't his usual setting.

The camerawoman had already been swallowed by the quickly shifting crowd, and the only sign of the mic operator was the boom he carried like a flag. He was trying to fight back towards Pablo, but the thin rake of a man could barely stand straight in the swirling rush of people. Jessica caught sight of her stiff-shouldered aunt heading back towards Askew Avenue—if the camera was gone, then so was she—and felt light and suddenly free.

"I'll be at my truck all afternoon," she called to Pablo with a wave. "Drop by if you want to see those new gadgets."

But before she'd pushed even a foot towards her truck, her nose tingled unmistakeably. She inhaled deeply, and the little bees everywhere made her senses swim with honey. Aha! That ingredient was what she needed to make her recipe a success, and she would detour to Just My Type and buy some with ease. She snaked among toddling bees, proud parents, and the swelling crowd awaiting the parade.

In the distance, she spotted a cluster of Pippa's siblings. The oldest, Madeline, beckoned her over, but Jessica couldn't stop. Not only did she need to get baking, but she wasn't going anywhere near the youngest Pankhurst sibling, Hattie. That girl had a knack for disaster Jessica wouldn't go near that day. She pointed towards Pippa's store and mouthed, "Later." Then, with relief, she stepped out of the busy village square onto Verse View.

She headed straight to Just My Type, already setting her mind into the calm meditation of baking. As she approached the three steps to the well-stocked shop, her eye caught a glint of red.

She leapt back, her instincts working far faster than her thoughts, which lingered in curiosity—what was the dripping crimson liquid, and why was it on the steps of her best friend's shop in the middle of the day?

Slowly, slowly, Jessica's thoughts caught up, and she understood what she was looking at. The bright-red liquid that oozed along the stone step could be only one thing: blood.

Jessica took another step back. Then she dropped her beloved Julia Child tote and stumbled. Her heel dropped off the pavement, and she fell into the empty road. The air was knocked from her lungs in a sharp but silent scream.

4

What had happened? Jessica was here only minutes ago. Now the shop's steps were covered in blood. And as her terrified gaze rose, she saw a smudged bright-red handprint on the door.

"Pippa," Jessica moaned. The voice in her head yelled the name, but only the faintest whisper passed her lips. What had happened to her best friend?

Pippa bubbled with more life than a freshly fed sourdough starter. She was lemon zest and smoked paprika—she was the boldest flavours in every part of Jessica's history. But where was she?

Jessica's shaking legs pushed her up, urging her to run away from this terrible scene. But she couldn't leave. She had to go inside. She needed to find—

"Pippa! You're OK!" Jessica stumbled once again as the door swung open and her friend appeared. Jessica grabbed the old elm tree she banged into and held on for dear life.

"Are you trying to scare my customers away?" Pippa asked, standing at the top of the steps. She didn't have a mark on her. No blood. In fact, the only hint of red about her was the patent pumps on her feet. "I don't know what strange habits you've picked up on the road, but screaming in the street still isn't the done thing in Little Quillington."

"I thought..." Jessica pointed down at the oozing trickle of blood. "I thought something had happened to you."

Pippa straightened. The three steps up to her shop made her tall enough to look down on Jessica for once. Her voice wavered slightly. "That must be a prank. You know how giddy kids get around the summer fête. This has to be fake blood."

Jessica pointed at the drips that continued down the road and led away from the village square. The bright liquid pooled on the pavement just a few metres away. That area was the entrance to Index Alley, and Jessica had a sinking feeling as she looked towards it. "I don't think so."

"Maybe someone..." Pippa stepped down carefully and clutched Jessica. "Maybe they..." The two women followed the droplets, and Pippa couldn't explain the worrying trail. Instead, she pulled out her phone and dialled 999. But she didn't press the call button, and as she looked up at Jessica, her eyes swam with hope.

A breeze carried the opening fanfare of the brass band from the square. People applauded, and children squealed. But to Jessica, the fête was a million miles away. Even the air felt colder where she was. Her limbs moved stiffly, as if winter had stolen through them, and it seemed to take an hour to reach the entrance to the alley.

"I can't look." Pippa covered her face. Jessica flashed back to their teenage horror-movie marathons, when Pippa had insisted she'd be fine this time then spent entire films buried behind a cushion.

Jessica squeezed her friend's shoulder and inhaled deeply. Then, she took the final step to the mouth of Index Alley alone.

Red. More red. That was all she saw. Red liquid that was no longer dribbled or splashed. Now, a pool of it glistened in the alley. And there, face down in the liquid, like a pear waiting to be poached, lay a pale and very still body.

The air around Jessica dropped another few degrees. This alley was colder than any walk-in freezer. Her bones felt like solid ice. Through shivering lips, she forced out the words, "Press Dial, Pippa. We need an ambulance." She took a deep breath. "I think we also need the police."

5

Jessica shivered as she turned back to Index Alley. It was shock, she knew, this feeling of frost in her veins. It made her want to run. But a person was lying on the ground, covered in blood, and there was a chance she could help. A slim chance, Jessica thought, looking at the ground slick with blood.

She tiptoed around the red stain and past heavy black shoes, faded blue jeans, and a thin white T-shirt that was swiftly turning maroon. At the person's head, she crouched down. She reached out a quavering hand. Her fingers stretched to the individual's T-shirt—its neck had been yanked to one side in the fall. She should straighten it, her shocked mind said. But Jessica caught herself. She shouldn't interfere with the scene.

Slowly, she inched her hand past the pulled fabric and pressed her fingers to the neck—to *his* neck, the stubble that scratched her knuckle suggested.

"I don't think he has a pulse," she said, trying and failing to make her words reach Pippa. Jessica leaned closer to press more firmly, wanting to be certain. "I can't find any—"

She froze. Her eyes caught a shape on his shoulder—the dark lines of a small tattoo. Only part of the image poked past the man's stretched collar, but a shot of familiarity rattled through her brain.

"The ambulance is five minutes away," Pippa called. "Is he still breathing?"

The tattoo on this shoulder was one she knew well. This man was Cameron, her main competition on the baking show. But why was he here?

Cameron came from London, hundreds of miles away. She'd last seen him a week earlier, storming through the crowd at a food festival and slamming the door of his truck. He'd just lost his spot in the contest by making a terrible mistake—swapping salt for sugar in a cake.

He'd shouted about it and thrown his sponge layers to the floor. "That's an amateur move. I'd never do that. Someone's sabotaged me, and I'm going to find out who."

The anger and bluster were typical for him. Every dropped spoon, timing disaster, and oven malfunction was someone else's fault, and he'd yelled at the cast and crew each week about it. He hadn't started out like that, of course. Cameron had held together enough episodes of cheeky charm and good humour to get viewers on his side and to convince several of the bakers to share their recipe plans with him. But when the competition got tougher, the cracks started to show.

Jessica looked down at his body. She still couldn't believe he'd ended up like this. Chefs were often an angry bunch, but very few of them wound up murdered. And that was what this had to be—murder—the trail of blood leading to a back-alley resting place pointed at that. But it was impossible to believe.

His death wasn't even the strangest thing about the situation. She had no idea what he was doing here in her hometown. From the looks of the blood trail, he'd been killed on the steps of her best friend's shop. He had no reason to be in this place. His presence didn't make sense, and her mind raced like a mixer on top speed as she fought to understand.

Jessica breathed deeply, trying to calm the panic coursing through her. Her worlds were colliding in the worst possible way.

She needed to get away from Cameron's body. She needed Pippa to tell her everything would be OK.

But as she turned back towards her best friend, Jessica caught the familiar glint of a camera lens. It was pointing directly at her, capturing her panic as she crowded over the body of her bitter baking rival.

6

"Jessica?" Pablo's eyes followed the blood trail along the alley straight to her, as though he could rewind the terrible scene. "What's happened?"

Jessica used every ounce of her strength to stand up and take a step towards him. The glint of the camera lens caught her eye again. Why was Pablo even here? She'd left him in the bustling square a few minutes earlier, and now he was back with his crew so he could... what? Was he planning to put this moment on TV? She waved her hands across his shot. No. Cut. He couldn't do this.

"Jessica, are you OK? What's happened here? Do you need help?"

She couldn't take in his questions. Her numb lips struggled to form words, but as she stumbled closer to Pablo, she regained her strength. "Stop. This isn't... entertainment." Her ears strained for the wail of sirens, but all they picked up were the cheerful pomp of the parade's brass band and the sugar-fuelled laughter of children.

Pablo stood between the camerawoman and the mic operator, blocking her exit from the alley. Jessica stretched to her full height and looked past him. Pippa was behind Pablo, her phone glued to her ear. Jessica caught the words "when" and "ambulance," and she prayed that the answer was "soon."

"Is that..." Though Pablo's voice was still small and distant, Jessica knew what he would ask. "Is that Cameron?"

AND THEN THERE WERE SCONES 25

Jessica nodded. She couldn't speak, but the three crew members clearly understood—they stared past her in wide-eyed horror.

This trio hadn't been part of the team recording the weekly challenges at food festivals. The crew hadn't even met Cameron, as far as she was aware. But everyone in the country knew "the tattooed bad boy of baking," as the papers loved to call him. His good looks and fiery temper had made him perfect front-page news. For the eight weeks he'd been in the contest, he was the most talked-about competitor.

The mic operator propped up his boom and clung to it like a crutch. The camerawoman shook so much she looked liable to drop her heavy equipment, and only her sturdy gloves helped her keep it firmly clutched to her shoulder. Pablo stood perfectly still, and Jessica couldn't tell what he was thinking.

"We should clear the area," the camerawoman said. "The ambulance will be here any minute."

But Pablo didn't listen. He grabbed the camerawoman's shoulder and steadied her, making sure she focused on Jessica.

The camerawoman was pale, and her legs looked weak. Filming something like this wasn't her job. She couldn't have expected such a grisly scene when she signed up for a baking-contest gig.

"You seem keen to get us out of here," Pablo said to Jessica. "What is it you don't want people to see?"

"I...No...I..." She just wanted to make space.

"As the prime suspect, it seems highly suspicious that you're so eager to get away."

"I'm not... not a suspect. I just found..." Jessica's voice was evading her once again. Why couldn't she gather words to explain?

"Cameron's your biggest rival in the contest."

She shook her head. For someone working on the programme, Pablo wasn't paying much attention to it. "He left the show last week. He's no longer in the competition."

Pablo nudged the camerawoman and whispered in her ear. The camera whirred, zooming in close enough to catch every quiver of Jessica's lips. Then Pablo stared so hard she felt the breath stop in her chest.

He said, "There's been an update from the production company, one which has been covered widely in the press this morning. They found out someone did in fact tamper with Cameron's ingredients. The crew member responsible has been fired. It's been on every front page today."

Jessica pressed a palm to the wall to steady herself. Could this be true? She'd been too busy hunting for butter to hear anything about it.

Cameron had shouted about being sabotaged, but nobody had really believed him. He was rash enough to mix up ingredients and sufficiently hot-headed that his angry reaction hadn't been surprising.

But Cameron was right. Someone really had ruined his cake and got him kicked off the show.

Pablo pushed the mic operator back into position and thrust the boom directly over Jessica's head. "Cameron was due to return to the contest next week." He paused and looked past her to the body in the alley. "That was the plan, anyway."

Jessica pressed a hand against her racing heart. This couldn't be happening.

Pablo waited for another, dramatic beat. "It looks like you're back in first place."

7

Jessica's legs trembled. Even the alley wall wobbled as she leaned against it. She was overworked dough—stretched and limp—her pale fingers melted into the bricks to which she tried to cling.

She wanted to run, but she could barely stand. And again, she saw the glint of the camera, capturing her reaction.

She looked over at Pippa, who was as white as milk and looked just as ready to spill in a puddle on the ground. She couldn't help.

Jessica shut her eyes, and a sharp wail pierced the dark uncertainty—the siren was closing in.

Again, her legs longed to run. Pablo was pointing the finger of suspicion straight at her. If he shared his ideas with the police, they'd slap handcuffs on her in an instant.

Panic flooded her thoughts. But along with the fear came a useful idea.

"What's Cameron doing here?" Jessica asked Pablo. "He's not from Little Quillington. He has no ties to the place. The only link is through the competition you work for. But he was off the show."

"Like I said, that decision has been overturned."

"And you knew that before I did. Was he brought here for some ratings-grabbing reveal?"

"The change was only announced this morning."

"It was *announced* then." Jessica wasn't even sure that part was true. She had no one's word for it but Pablo's. "But as a crew member, you must have known about it earlier. Did you bring Cameron here to have some on-camera confrontation with me?" Until a couple of months earlier, Jessica would never have believed how fake situations on TV were. But now her eyes were wide open.

"His presence in Little Quillington is as much of a surprise to me as it is to you."

"You were here with a camera crew just moments after I discovered his body. That's a little too convenient. Are *you* trying to hide something?"

He thumbed to a sign behind him. "We were escaping the crowds by following these arrows and—"

Before he could finish, someone laid a hand on his shoulder and pulled him away. Jessica was swept from the alley, too, as a pair of paramedics rushed to Cameron.

Jessica raced to Pippa's side, and she clung to her friend as she watched the paramedics crouch down and feel Cameron's neck. Despite their youthful appearances, their dark green uniforms and large bags of medical equipment were reassuring. This was all going to be OK.

But then the pimple-cheeked man checking for a pulse shook his head. He laced his fingers while his colleague turned Cameron over, and together, the pair administered chest compressions and pumped air into him.

Jessica held her own breath. Her body was as still and controlled as when she piped delicate flowers onto cupcakes. She focused just as intensely on Cameron, willing him to be OK. Perhaps her inexpert skills had simply missed the signs of life. Any second now, he would sit up and shout about her silly mistake.

But the paramedics slowed then stopped. They checked once more for a pulse that was long gone. Then they packed up their equipment.

No. That couldn't be it.

Jessica looked over to the film crew. The camerawoman was still clutching her enormous camera as tightly as she would a security blanket.

Pablo reached out to pat the mic operator's shaking shoulder. The grey-haired man was as tall and spindly as the boom pole he carried. At Pablo's touch, he sagged into the director's arms. Pablo looked shocked—the crew didn't seem close enough for hugs—but he held his lanky colleague, who looked overcome by the unbelievable turn of events.

Pablo patted his associate's back stiffly until the older man straightened, wiped his face, and stepped away. The mic operator clutched his boom pole as he turned to Jessica.

"Sorry for—"

"No!" Pippa cried beside her.

Jessica turned to her friend. Now wasn't the time for fighting.

But Pippa wasn't shouting at him. She wasn't even looking in his direction. Instead, she was facing the village square, which could just be seen at the end of the street. She raised a trembling finger towards it and cried out once again. "No!"

In the distance, the crowds were clearing. When Jessica saw why, she understood what made Pippa so upset.

8

At the end of Verse View, in the village square, a tiny, jelly-legged bee toddled across the grass. The child wore yellow tights, a stripy leotard, and wings made of cut-up bed sheets tied at her shoulders and wrists. She also bore, on top of her head, a fuzzy pipe-cleaner crown that could only mean one thing. This girl was the queen bee, the one chosen by the Askew family board to lead the parade—and every person following it—along the route to the summer fête.

Any minute now, at least a hundred other toddlers would follow, then the float carrying Sherlock Holmes, and finally, the brass band that would call everyone to come along for the fun.

They would all trail the bold little girl in front, who had been trained for weeks to follow the arrows of this year's route.

Pippa's sharp cry of "No!" and her pointing finger were aimed at just one thing—the arrow leading directly down Verse View and past Index Alley.

Jessica saw the ingredients laid out before her—the innocent toddlers, the trusting parade, and the grisly murder scene. It was a recipe for disaster.

"You do directions; I'll do distractions." Jessica's eyes darted so rapidly between the oncoming parade and her pale-faced best friend that she felt faint. They'd done this once before, as kids, and she prayed Pippa remembered.

Pippa hesitated. Then she took a deep breath and ran towards the lamppost on the edge of Verse View. An arrow was tied to it. She leapt up and batted it with her palm, directing the route along the edge of the village square. The crowd was now close enough that several dozen people saw the action, but Pippa had perfected a cheery smile when she and Jessica did this as teens, one that said Pippa was happy to help, even though this change was awfully last-minute. The act was easier to pull off as an adult, since what woman in her thirties would change a parade route without good reason?

The next part was a little harder for Pippa. She had to race down Verse View and collect several arrows to tie onto a new route. Going faster than the toddler leading the parade wouldn't be tricky. But moving fast enough to avoid being caught by Aunt Enriqueta before she'd finished would be a challenge. The black-clad woman stood at the end of Askew Avenue, watching the event like a hawk.

This point was, unfortunately, where Jessica came in. She had to create enough of a distraction that none of the Askews on the square would look Pippa's way.

The little bee leading the parade crouched to examine a daisy growing through a crack in the paving. Onlookers cooed at the adorable scene, giving Jessica and Pippa precious extra moments.

Jessica looked around for an effective distraction. If she was in her food truck, she could pop open the hatch and serve cookies to draw the crowd her way. That would easily annoy her aunt enough for her to miss the moving of arrows in the square. But the truck was parked several streets away, precisely to avoid her relatives' attention.

She considered, for a fear-filled moment, simply going over to her skeleton-thin aunt and picking her up. Running off with the woman slung over her shoulder would certainly distract everyone. But there had to be a better option than that.

Then she spotted the man dressed as a beekeeper, who was meant to keep the events running smoothly. The man carried a full pint of beer in each fist, and he was weaving over from the Quill and Well pub. He was the perfect target for the distraction portion of her plan.

Jessica looked over her shoulder to check on Pippa. She was already approaching the square, carrying two arrows, and she would dart ahead of the ambling queen bee to lay out the new route at any moment.

Pushing through the crowd, Jessica darted around benches and trees, and hopped over the many dogs, children, and piles of shopping people had with them. She was panting when she reached the wobbling man dressed as a beekeeper.

Jessica bent over beside him, looking for all the world as though she were merely catching her breath. Then she hooked a foot around his ankle and yanked. The drunk man fell in slow motion, sending great arcs of beer across the crowd and grabbing a sunburned boy and a skimpily dressed woman on the way down. These two clutched on to others, and the falling, beer-soaked mob yelled and cried so loudly that every eye turned to them in an instant.

In the distance, Pippa strung up the newly located arrows, directing the parade away from Verse View. And not a single person noticed.

As people slowly turned back towards the queen bee and her trailing retinue, they parted like the Red Sea, opening up the route slowly but surely. By the time the parade turned onto Askew Avenue, it was too late for anyone to stop it.

Several book buyers with their noses in new purchases looked surprised by sudden obstacles in their path, and Aunt

Enriqueta backed away from the oncoming horde with an expression of disbelief, but there was no other problem with the direction the children took.

Jessica waved to Pippa, who disappeared in the distance to continue putting up arrows along the new route and ensure everyone reached the final destination of the fête. Jessica longed to follow and stick close to her friend. After the morning's terrible fright, she wanted nothing more than to lose herself in eating ice creams, playing hook-a-duck, and getting her face painted. She wanted to be a child again, enjoying the summer fun with her best friend, even if just for a day.

But she couldn't do any of that. She needed to make it clear to Pablo and his crew that she hadn't fled the scene without reason. He'd pointed the finger of accusation at her very quickly. She needed to stop him repeating his suspicions to the police.

Jessica pushed against the tide of the crowd to head towards Verse View. But as she got closer to it, a strobing blue light and wailing siren said she was too late.

Then she spotted something even worse in the crowd, and her body stiffened like well-whipped cream.

9

"It's him! I saw it with my own eyes. Didn't realise who it was at first, but..."

Jessica couldn't hear the man's next words, but she knew what they'd be about. He was dressed in the distinctive dark green of a paramedic, and she recognised his plump, pimply cheeks. This man was one of the pair who'd crouched down in Index Alley and shaken their heads over Cameron's body.

Now he was standing by the ornate bench on which Mr Hoffman, the librarian, was sitting with his family. Indeed, the red-faced paramedic was speaking to one of Mr Hoffman's daughters. Jessica didn't know the young woman, who was a decade younger than her and had been a kid when she left the village. But she knew the woman's name. This was Lydia, the youngest of the Hoffman girls, all five of whom were named for the Bennet sisters in *Pride and Prejudice*.

Jessica also recognised the expression on Lydia's face. She was bursting with excitement to share the gossip she'd just heard. But the young ambulance worker wouldn't let her go just yet. He had something else to tell, and he leaned in extremely close to share it.

The hairs on the back of Jessica's neck prickled. This couldn't be happening. The medical professional surely wasn't sharing details of the patient he'd just tried and failed to revive. Even in the small village of Little Quillington, the laws against doing so applied.

But Lydia shut her eyes to relish the news, and Jessica knew that the paramedic had thrown the rules to the wind for a chance to get close to the pretty girl. Jessica also knew exactly where Lydia would look when she opened her enchanting eyes.

Straight at her.

Lydia's shocked expression sparkled with eagerness, and after she'd scrutinised Jessica for signs of the drama the young paramedic had just shared, she turned to her closest sister. All the Hoffman girls had glossy, dark hair they wore in thick plaits. These flicked like whips as the sisters shared the sordid tale, and each one in turn looked at Jessica with shock.

She wished she were close enough to hear exactly what they were whispering. The sparkles in the girls' eyes said it was about more than her discovery of Cameron's body. The paramedic had also told them of Pablo's accusation.

"No," Jessica moaned. But she could only look on with the same helplessness as when she watched a cake overflowing its tin in the oven.

Gossip travelled the square faster than a pinch of icing sugar in the wind.

"...in Index Alley? Was it..."

"Dead? But he's my favourite. And he's so..."

"...said that temper of his would get him in trouble, didn't I?"

"Apparently she was covered in blood, so it certainly looks like Jessica Askew was..."

"...got a history, and it can't be a coincidence that she..."

Jessica wanted to snatch the words from the air. But they were flying too quickly, and sly looks shot across the square with them. Face after face turned to her with suspicion.

"And after he got kicked off the show, too, poor lad. Things couldn't get any worse for him."

"Well, no, Mary. He's dead. I'd say that's about as bad as can be."

This pair of voices was right behind her. Jessica glanced over her shoulder and recognised regulars from her grandma's shop. They were standing mere inches away, talking about Cameron's death like a storyline in their favourite soap opera.

"And that girl," said the older woman, who wore the same stiff bob and thick mascara she did when Jessica was little, "her aunt always said she was trouble. And now look, she's murdered a lad in cold blood."

Jessica spun around. She gave the women a look a sharp as her kitchen knives.

"I tried to help him," she said. "I was the one who found him, and I called for help. That's all that happened. I didn't do anything to hurt Cameron."

Then she pushed past the open-mouthed women and through the chattering crowd.

Sweat trickled down Jessica's neck as eyes burned into her from every side. She could barely breathe as she felt the attention press in tighter. She needed to get away.

But even if she did, that wouldn't help. The story wouldn't stop here. News of Cameron's death and her discovery of the body would already have zipped far and wide. She almost choked on the taste of the whispers and the throng of digital messages that travelled through the warm air, all spreading tales about her.

The social-media storm after every episode of the baking show had been swift and powerful. Contestants had been brought to tears over responses to the shapes of their cookies and their choice of sprinkle colours on a cupcake. Jessica had experienced this negativity the week her sponge came out as flat as a pancake. *Failure. Waste of space. My dog could do better.* What would people say when they thought she was a killer?

Her phone felt hot in her right pocket. She didn't dare look at it, but she knew what sorts of words would be on there when the gossip spread beyond this village square. *Body. Suspect. Murder.*

Jessica hadn't done anything, but could she prove it? Cameron must have been killed in the brief window between her two visits to Just My Type. She'd been on camera for most of that time. But not all of it.

To make matters worse, she seemed like the obvious culprit. She and Cameron had fought several times.

Then Pablo had found her crouching over Cameron's body, and yes, Pippa could explain she'd discovered, not murdered, him. But what was a friend's word against evidence on film? She knew by now how edits could seal a person's fate.

Jessica hadn't done anything wrong, but would anyone believe her?

As she pushed to the edge of the square, she saw two stern faces that clearly didn't. A pair of police officers was heading her way. Their fingers dangled by their duty belts, itching to pull out handcuffs and cart her to jail.

Jessica's legs once more pulsed with the urge to run. It wasn't too late to dive back into the crowd. She knew this village well, and she could still escape.

But instead, she headed right towards the officers. She returned their hard stare, showing that she wasn't afraid.

She hadn't killed Cameron, and she would prove it.

10

"Where on earth have you been?"

Those sharp words made the police officers flinch, and Jessica tensed too. She spun and saw who was shouting—Aunt Enriqueta, whose dark clothing added an extra layer of menace.

Jessica shuffled into the thinning edge of the crowd, her instincts pushing her away. At six feet tall, though, it was impossible for her to hide. She took a deep breath and squared her shoulders, ready to face the black-clad woman.

But Aunt Enriqueta wasn't talking to her. The woman's anger was directed at the police officers, who she strode so close to they took a step back.

"You ought to have been here hours ago." Aunt Enriqueta poked the closest officer's thick tactical vest. "The Askew board gave ample notice that the village's resident officer would be away this weekend and that replacements were required from first thing this morning."

Jessica couldn't believe her aunt was speaking like this to an officer of the law. Jabbing his chest was surely an arrestable offence.

"Ma'am, we're here to—" the older one started, taking another step back.

"You are here to keep the crowds in order, and so far, you have done an abysmal job."

"We're not here for crowd control," the older officer boomed loudly enough to stop a thief in their tracks.

His voice rattled Jessica's bones, and her shoulders squeezed in tightly. But Aunt Enriqueta didn't so much as flicker her eyelids.

"The force doesn't provide police support for events this small," the younger man said. Then he stood stiffly to attention as though expecting a gold star. Despite wearing the same high-hitched trousers, perfectly polished boots, and clipped moustache as his colleague, this officer looked to be on his first day on the job, while the other was perhaps hours from retirement.

"Do not blindly quote regulations at me, young man. The village of Little Quillington has a centuries-old arrangement with the constabulary to manage the crowds we attract to the region." Aunt Enriqueta looked down her nose at the officer, and though they were the same height, he shrivelled. "In your absence, there has already been a significant catastrophe. Our meticulously planned parade was rerouted by hooligans, whom I sincerely hope you plan on punishing."

For a moment, Jessica thought her aunt didn't know that she, Jessica, had changed the direction of the parade. But then the woman turned to her with a look as bitter as burnt coffee. Jessica's stomach churned loudly.

"There has been utter chaos, thanks to the miscreants responsible. As the parade is now running along a cobbled road, several visitors in unsuitable shoes have twisted their ankles, a gentleman in a wheelchair has been extremely jostled, and we have had to separate the Sherlock Holmes float and send it on to the fête alone."

Jessica forced herself to step out from the edge of the crowd. "I can explain everything."

But Aunt Enriqueta wasn't finished. "The reputational damage caused by today's disaster will also significantly impact Little Quillington's commercial future. I would like you to arrest the person responsible for—"

The older officer held up a hand to stop her, and Aunt Enriqueta's cheeks blazed red enough to catch flame. Nobody ever dared silence her. But then she saw the officer turn sharply towards Jessica, and her thin lips curved like the mouth of the cat who'd got the cream.

Explanations about queen bees and dead bakers tumbled together in Jessica's brain, and she knew how crazy she would sound.

The older officer's neat moustache twitched. "We've been looking for you, young lady. Why don't you tell us what happened down Index Alley and what exactly your relationship was to the deceased?"

11

Jessica couldn't speak.

"We understand you had a prior connection with the victim," the young officer said, mirroring his partner's hard glare.

That line was right out of the novels Aunt Enriqueta sold in Criminally Good Mysteries, and to hear it spoken aloud in the village square made the black-clad woman look like a stiff breeze could sweep her off her feet.

"His name's Cameron," Jessica said quietly, needing to steer the events from the realm fiction and into reality. "I've only known him for a few weeks. We're on a baking show together."

"And you invited him here this weekend?"

She risked a glance at Aunt Enriqueta, who had quickly recovered from her shock and was smiling in satisfaction, as though she'd suspected all along that Jessica would end up embroiled in murder scandal.

Jessica shook her head. She clutched the cuffs of her linen shirt and reached up to straighten the straps of her tote bag. But the bag wasn't there. She couldn't recall having had it for a while, in fact. Maybe not since she'd returned to Just My Type for honey. Where had it gone? She felt a trace of her earlier desperation for butter and then longed to return to the time when its absence was her biggest problem.

"Miss?" the older police officer said sharply. "My colleague asked you a question. Are you able to provide an explanation for the presence of the deceased in village this weekend?"

She shook her head again. She couldn't explain anything that had happened that day. Cameron's presence in Little Quillington was as strange as stirring chilli flakes into cherry pie.

Whispers thickened around her, making it clear that everyone else had plenty of theories. But Jessica had nothing to say.

The sound of a click from a nearby camera made her jump. Then she noticed several phones pointed in her direction. She opened her mouth to ask the officers if they could have this conversation in private. But doing that would mean the police station—and possibly handcuffs and lawyers and matters so official she felt faint. She straightened her spine and reminded herself she'd done nothing wrong.

"Cameron and I have been on a weekly baking programme together for the last couple of months." She spoke loudly, knowing that people would be recording for social media or even for material to sell to the papers. "He left the competition last week, and I didn't expect to see him again. This morning, after filming a segment for the show with my aunt"—Jessica paused and looked at the woman, making it clear that if she was being railroaded into suspicion, she wouldn't go alone—"I walked down Verse View and discovered a trail of blood. I followed it and found Cameron on the ground in Index Alley. I couldn't find his pulse, so I called an ambulance right away. But it was too late to save him."

Her voice trembled as the reality of the situation hit her. Cameron was dead. The people standing nearby, hoping to hear the latest twist in the day's gossip, bowed their heads and stepped back. She'd performed enough grief to earn their pity, it seemed.

But there wasn't a flicker of pity from Aunt Enriqueta. In fact, her expression said she'd long suspected Jessica would end up in a situation like this. Aunt Enriqueta's face also said she couldn't wait to tell the rest of the family.

When Jessica thought of her beloved grandma hearing the news, she couldn't breathe. A python of panic wrapped around her, squeezing her lungs so tightly she felt faint. Just a few moments earlier, she'd been certain she should stand her ground and tell the police the truth. But that seemed foolish now. She was the most obvious suspect in Cameron's death—she was the only link to the village where he'd been killed. Who else would they consider when they could simply lock her up and throw away the key?

But just then, she spotted something. It was the flash of a woman's hair—thick chestnut waves with pastel pink tips. The sight was a mere flicker in the distance, but she knew exactly who the hair belonged to, and she had to follow it.

She hesitated a moment, straining for words to explain. But there was no time. Instead, she turned to the flowing hair, fixed her focus on it like the last step in a recipe, and ran.

12

This hair could belong to only one person—Leah, the pretty, young baker who was just behind Jessica in the TV contest. At least part of her success was down to these beautiful locks, from which she removed two large clips at the end of each day before shaking out her luxurious waves that charmed viewers and judges alike.

Right then, Leah's hair flew like a flag, announcing to the world that she was here in Little Quillington. Just like Cameron, she had no reason to be in the village. Her presence couldn't be a coincidence.

Leah was fast on her feet, slipping around the thinning crowd in the square and hopping over planters and freshly planted saplings. She was almost a decade younger than Jessica, whose body instantly told her to stop this sprinting nonsense and sit down for a rest. But Jessica couldn't give up her only lead in Cameron's death. Her hopes were as fragile as meringue, but they were all she had. As she swerved around the ice cream cart, she realised she did have one other thing—local knowledge. Leah didn't know Little Quillington at all, however, and that was about to become a problem.

The young woman darted towards the shops lining the east side of the square and ran in front of To Brie or Not to Brie. The cheese shop opened at twelve thirty exactly, and the nearby church bell told Jessica to swerve as she approached. Leah continued running, unaware. When the shop door flung open with a bang, she was unprepared for the full conviction with which its owner, Wystan Finney, stepped into her path. Leah ran into him with a cartoonish, shuddering thud.

Wystan the cheesemonger was utterly unaffected. In fact, he barely noticed. The sturdy barrel of a man proceeded with the opening routine he'd held for decades and recited a fragment of poetry to a tune of his own devising. That day, he chose his favourite, a short stanza by WH Auden, with whom he shared a first name. Wystan bellowed the lines in his thick Welsh accent, his cheeks pink with relish: "A poet's hope: to be, / like some valley cheese, / local, but prized elsewhere."

Leah tumbled to the hard flagstones at his feet. She lay dazed, which surely had as much to do with the fragrance of pungent cheese as her bump into the man who sold it.

But then Leah looked up and spotted Jessica, who stood mere metres away. Leah's face was filled with a waxen, nightmare-like fear—an expression that said Jessica was the last person she wanted to see.

She leapt up and sped back into the thinning end of the crowd that was drifting behind the parade. If she moved with them down Askew Avenue, she would emerge at the far end into moorland. This open expanse of moody landscape stretched into seeming infinity. The moors around Little Quillington were the ones run through by the lovers in *Wuthering Heights*, and those environs surrounded both Mary Lennox's secret garden and Nicholas Nickelby's brutal boarding school. The rolling hills looked wide and featureless, but a person could disappear into them with ease.

Jessica couldn't let that happen. Leah was her only lead. She leapt over a flower border of red and white roses, swung around a Narnia-style lamppost, and hurdled the prone body of a tantrum-throwing child to close the distance between her and Leah. Then she followed her onto Askew Avenue.

The road here was made of setts—rectangular cobblestones that Jessica knew so well she could walk them blindfolded. Leah, however, was a stranger in Little Quillington, and she stumbled almost instantly. She staggered, but didn't fall, and she gave no sign of tiring.

Jessica's heart was ready to leap out of her chest, and her lungs were screaming with effort. She couldn't keep going like this. She had to stop Leah before she got further ahead.

Jessica leapt towards the small baker and threw her full force behind the tackle, knowing that her own entire future could very well be at stake.

13

Years of whisking had strengthened Jessica's grip. Though her fingertips barely grazed the hem of Leah's top, she clutched hard and refused to let go. Her sharp yank made Leah stop in midair like a cartoon character two feet from a cliff. Then the young baker fell to the ground with a thud.

This time, when Leah landed, she stayed down. The fall knocked the air from Jessica's lungs, and she panted hard as she kept an eye on the runaway.

Parade stragglers looked down at the sprawled women but were too focused on getting to the fête to really care.

"Stop...running..." Jessica gasped. "Please."

Leah said nothing. She merely sat in a tight ball with her arms wrapped around her.

Jessica pressed a hand to her chest as she struggled up too. Then she shuffled to the curb to gather enough breath and finally ask, "What are you doing here?"

"I... I'm..."

Jessica peered through Leah's flowing chestnut waves and was surprised to see the other woman's face was wet with tears. "You're what?"

"Is he really dead?" Leah's voice was barely a whisper. "I... I heard someone say it in the square, but I couldn't believe it. Then I saw the paramedic, and I just knew. Cameron's gone."

For a moment, Jessica's chest swelled with concern—it bubbled up as swiftly as boiling milk—but she pushed the feeling away.

"You know he's dead." Her voice was hard and cold. She dusted off her bruised legs and stretched them gingerly. "You're the one who killed him."

"No, I..." Leah shook her head, making her long hair wave in the breeze.

"That's why you ran, isn't it?" She stared at Leah and chewed the inside of her lip to keep still while adrenaline raced through her at lightning speed. The young woman before her looked far too frail for murder, but what other explanation could there be? Neither she nor Cameron had any reason to be here in Little Quillington, and now one of them was dead.

"No, I was upset. I realised what had happened, and I just had to get away." Leah sniffed then rubbed her damp face. "I shouldn't have run. I was in a daze, and when you chased me, I panicked."

"What are you even doing here? Is the plan to kill me next?" Jessica hadn't considered that possibility until the words sprang out. But it made sense. The only thing connecting Cameron, Leah, and the village was Jessica. Had Leah lured Cameron here to kill her two biggest rivals in one weekend?

Leah shook her head, her deep chestnut curls wafting like she had a personal wind machine. Her eyes became even wider than usual. "The production company sent me. Didn't Pablo tell you? My family lives in Spain, but the contest didn't want to send a crew there. I have some friends nearby that Pablo interviewed, and he thought it would be good if I came here for a head-to-head challenge with you. He didn't mention that?"

Jessica had heard nothing about this. Could Leah be telling the truth? Jessica wanted to believe it—the explanation was better than someone trying to kill her, and springing a surprise challenge was just the sort of thing the production company would do. But she couldn't lower her guard when a killer was on the loose.

She slowly pushed herself up to her feet. She was tired from the intense few weeks of the competition. This chase and tumble on the cobbles had been the last thing she needed. "Nobody said anything."

"The producers thought it would boost ratings," Leah added, sniffling as she, too, struggled back to a standing position. "Cameron came here to support me, since I didn't have any family around, and... Oh... who cares about any of it now that... that Cameron is gone?"

Jessica reached out to steady Leah, whose shoulders shook violently as she burst into fresh sobs. But then Jessica pulled back. She wasn't sure Leah's story was true. And there was another reason to hesitate.

Now Jessica looked down from her full height. "Cameron has argued with every contestant and crew member on the show, yourself included. After what he said about your apple crumble last episode, I don't know why you're crying over him."

Although she was surprised by the sharpness of her words, she was speaking the truth. She'd been shocked to find Cameron's body, but she hadn't shed a tear about it. Leah's reaction was looking suspicious.

Leah gazed up with doe eyes overflowing with tears. "His meanness was an act. He was making good TV so he could have a career after all this. But that wasn't the real him. He's... We're... I love him."

14

Leah *loved* Cameron. She loved that thorn in everyone's side—that snake in the grass. How was that possible? Could he really be a nice guy?

Jessica had barely processed Leah's words—and she certainly hadn't got close to understanding them—when a pair of heavy boots thudded down Askew Avenue and stopped beside her.

"I hope you've got a good explanation for running from the police," said the young officer, who straightened his spine, puffed up his chest and looked Jessica in the eye. Away from his older colleague, he seemed like a child playing dress-up. Her fingers itched to tug his moustache and see if it was stuck on.

"I was following Leah," Jessica said. She opened her mouth to explain who Leah was and to share her suspicions about her involvement in Cameron's death. But she was still dazed by the young woman's confession of love. All Jessica could manage was, "She knew Cameron as well."

"Oh... I... I didn't see you there, miss," the young officer said, his Adam's apple bobbing nervously in his long neck. Apparently, no introductions were needed. "I've watched you every week. I'm a big fan."

Leah beamed and blinked her damp lashes. She softly murmured, "Thank you."

"She was running," Jessica blurted, "so I chased her." Sourness as sharp as vinegar pinched in her chest when she said this, but Leah's story was suspect. The pretty young woman couldn't simply smile and escape interrogation by the police.

"I *was* running," Leah said, nodding vigorously. "I'm very sorry, officer. I know I should have come to find you as soon as I heard what happened, but I was so upset."

"It's a common reaction," the policeman said, nodding sagely and slipping into a wide-legged stance, his hands resting on his duty belt. "Perfectly understandable."

Jessica had not received such understanding that day. This officer especially had looked as though he longed to shove her in a cell and throw away the key. But Jessica clamped her lips over a complaint about his treatment of her. Leah's popularity had bought Jessica a little breathing room, and she wouldn't risk losing that.

Leah pulled out her phone and held up the lockscreen. On it was a selfie of Cameron with his arm slung around Leah's shoulders. "This was the last photo we took together. I just... I can't believe it."

Jessica peered at the image. In the background, she recognised the heart-shaped pink double doors of Kiss and Tale, the specialist romance shop just a few metres away, which was owned by Aunt Jo and her daughter Iris. The bright blue summer fête bunting at the very edge of the shot said the picture had been taken earlier that day.

The idea of Cameron and Leah together still made no sense. It was as strange as pouring honey over burned toast—her sweetness couldn't overpower his dark, fiery temper. But Leah had said his angry side was an act. Given all Jessica had learned about the world of TV, she was tempted to believe that. Perhaps his bad attitude really had been for the press. If so, it had worked. He'd been called the next Gordon Ramsey, and rumours abounded that he was releasing his own recipe book and would star in a solo TV show to go with it.

As a breeze cooled the sweat on her brow and sent a tingle down the back of her neck, Jessica realised how full of adrenaline she'd been. Now it had burned off, the thought of Leah as a ruthless killer seemed crazy. She was just a young girl in love.

"I'm terribly sorry for your loss, miss," the young police officer said, a little more tenderly than seemed professional. "We've not got any official word on what happened to your young man. By which I mean, I don't want to be questioning anyone for the time being. You must need some time to come to terms with everything. I'll take your details and get in touch if we want to speak about anything."

Jessica had seen Cameron in the alley. Surely, no "official word" was needed to know he'd been murdered. There'd been blood everywhere. But again, she clenched her teeth to keep from putting herself in the frame. If the officer's affection for Leah meant he wouldn't shine a light in Jessica's eyes any time soon, that was fine by her.

"Thank you," Leah murmured, looking at the officer from beneath her long lashes. She wrote her details in his notebook.

"I'm Billy, by the way," he said, keeping his gaze fixed on Leah as he passed the small black book to Jessica. She was nearly certain she could get away with scrawling nonsense instead of her real name and number, but she figured doing so would come back to bite her in the long run.

Leah pulled her hair into a ponytail. "Thank you for being so understanding, Billy. Please let me know if you have any news about what happened."

"Will do, miss." He wiped his damp hand on his trousers before reaching out to her for a shake. Then he stepped back and looked at both women. "And, as I said, I'll be in touch if we've got any questions."

Jessica forced a smile, trying not to feel bitter that his last comment was clearly aimed at her. The smile dropped the moment he turned and walked away. She wanted to be happy that she was out from under the police's gaze for the time being. But young Officer Billy had just taken down the details of the two best suspects in Cameron's murder and waved them away. Her stomach grumbled with unease at the realisation of how little use the police would be in solving this case.

In the eyes of the press and everyone in Little Quillington, she was the prime suspect. If the police weren't going to find the real culprit, she'd have to do it herself.

15

Jessica watched the police officer as he walked across the village square and out of sight. Only then did she let her tense shoulders drop a fraction of an inch.

This relaxation was a mistake. Seconds later, she was drowning in syrup-thick waves of worry about who had killed Cameron, whether the baking show was cancelled, what the cancellation would mean for her food truck's future, why Leah and Cameron were really in Little Quillington, and who was watching her right then. That last thought made her skin prickle. She was standing on Askew Avenue, a street where every shop was owned by a member of her family.

Right then, she was surely being observed. Jessica looked at Criminally Good Mysteries, the shop she and Leah were standing before. But Aunt Enriqueta couldn't be there—Jessica had seen her in the village square only minutes ago, and she hadn't passed by since then. Still, the woman would return at some point, and Jessica didn't want to be here when she did.

She turned to Leah. "We should—"

But the young woman wasn't listening. She let out a loud sob and sat heavily on the front step of Criminally Good Mysteries, the last place Jessica wanted to be. She needed to get Leah out of here before she drew any further attention.

"Is your truck nearby?" Jessica hadn't seen the pretty teal-and-gold food truck in the village that morning. Leah's business focused on macarons, and an enormous model of one was mounted on her roof, making the truck very hard to miss. Perhaps Jessica could walk Leah there and look for clues about the events of that morning. Somehow, somewhere, there had to be an answer about what had happened to Cameron.

"I can't believe he's gone!" Leah wailed. She looked truly devastated, but this situation was still hard for Jessica to understand.

Her mind filled with a long list of everyone Cameron had argued with in the few weeks she'd known him. He'd found fault with each member of the cast and crew, and he hadn't been afraid to show it. Nobody on the list had a link to Little Quillington, though, so they provided no hints about where to look for Cameron's killer.

As Jessica tried to think of any other leads, Leah's sobs quietened slightly.

From her perch on the front step of Criminally Good Mysteries, Leah pulled up her knee socks and tightened her ponytail. Then she noticed how dirty her pretty white cardigan was where she'd tumbled to the ground in it. As Leah removed her cardigan and brushed the dust away, Jessica spotted something on the young woman's pale shoulder. It was a tattoo—one she recognised. The design was the small, neat line drawing of a whisk.

Jessica had seen the same tattoo very recently—on Cameron's shoulder. She'd seen it streaked with blood when she'd found his body in the alley. His whisk looked identical to the tattoo's design. He and Leah were matching-tattoo levels of seriousness.

"Who could..." Leah ran her fingers under her lashes, wiping away the faint smudge of her makeup. "Who could have done this to him?"

AND THEN THERE WERE SCONES 57

Jessica shook her head. She truly had no idea, but she prayed she'd find out soon, not just for Leah's sake but her own. Gossip moved swiftly in Little Quillington, and it wouldn't take long for news of the murder to reach her grandma's ears. With it would come whispers about Jessica's role. She couldn't let that happen.

"We can work this out together," Jessica said. "There's nothing but bookshops on this street. Let's head back to the square and get a cup of tea."

She held out her hand, eager to get away from her family's gaze.

When the door behind Leah flew open, however, Jessica realised she was too late.

16

"This isn't a park bench," snapped Aunt Enriqueta. "Remove yourselves from the entrance to my shop."

Jessica pulled Leah up, and the two women darted backwards over cobblestones. Where had Aunt Enriqueta come from? Her shop was the only one on the street without a back door, and she couldn't have slipped by Jessica unnoticed.

Aunt Enriqueta was named for Enriqueta Rylands, founder of the beautiful John Rylands library in Manchester. But Aunt Enriqueta had neither that woman's generosity nor her temperament for libraries. Jessica's aunt was a woman whose presence was hard to miss.

"Sorry," Leah murmured as she once again wiped her damp face.

Jessica said nothing. She was still confused about where her aunt had come from.

"I do not know what you think you are doing here, but your obstruction is damaging my business." Aunt Enriqueta's scorn was as cold as a walk-in freezer. "Have you not done enough harm for one day?"

Jessica looked down at her aunt's shoes, realising there was only one way she could have arrived unnoticed. The tops of her black boots were polished to a mirror-like shine. But their soles were caked in damp, pale clay. This material wasn't the heavy peat of the moors but another distinctive local dirt, a kind that came from deep underground, from the tunnels that ran beneath every building on this street, connecting the Askews' bookshops and known only by the family.

Aunt Enriqueta must have snuck in through the back of another shop, descended a hidden flight of stairs, walked the dimly lit tunnel network, and climbed up into her own business. For what? Just to jump out at Jessica like this?

Jessica refused to give her what she wanted. She stayed silent and did not react.

Her inaction brought pink spots of anger back to her aunt's cheeks. Jessica tugged at Leah, who was brushing down her white cotton dress. Jessica took her arm and tried to lead her away. But Leah's steps were heavy with grief.

"And you can tell that no-good man you were here with that he is not welcome in my shop ever again," Aunt Enriqueta said.

Jessica stumbled on the familiar cobblestones. What was her aunt talking about? Jessica hadn't been in her shop for years. But then she glanced at Aunt Enriqueta and saw she was pointing at Leah.

Jessica recalled the photo on Leah's lockscreen—she and Cameron had been on Askew Avenue that morning. And it sounded like they'd visited Criminally Good Mysteries. Jessica's mind scrambled to fit those details into what she understood about the day.

Cameron had clearly done something to make Aunt Enriqueta angry. That wasn't hard, though he seemed to have done an especially good job of it. Aunt Enriqueta didn't usually shout in the street, not in front of potential customers. He must have done something she considered truly terrible to warrant that. But what? Jessica's curiosity was as insatiable as her sweet tooth.

The pale clay on her boots said Aunt Enriqueta was hiding something—there was no good reason for her to sneak into her own shop.

Jessica's mind stretched taut as she tried to make sense of all this.

There were too many ingredients that didn't fit into a single recipe. Jessica needed more information. She hooked her arm through Leah's and walked her around the quiet perimeter of the village square. Plenty of people were still milling on the grass in the middle—enjoying ice creams, waiting for friends, or simply avoiding the busy start of the summer fête—but the shops around the edge were enjoying the calm after the storm of the parade.

"I'm sorry about my aunt," Jessica said. This wasn't the first time she'd apologised for the woman. "What happened between her and Cameron? Did she..." Jessica paused, not entirely sure what she was trying to say.

Before she could put her thoughts into words, she caught sight of a figure heading their way. It was Pablo, taking the typical TV jog that was no faster than walking but looked busy.

"I've just had confirmation from production. Your head-to-head is still on for tomorrow." His voice was loud enough to catch the attention of several people nearby. "The permits can't be amended, so it's now or never, unfortunately. Every sympathy, though, of course."

What? This is madness. Hot coals of anger burned in Jessica's chest, but before she said anything, she looked around for a camera. Doing so had become a habit over recent weeks, and it was fortunate too. Jogging just a foot behind Pablo were the camerawoman and mic operator, both carrying their cumbersome equipment over the flagstones with ease.

"We can't keep going like nothing's happened." Jessica's presentable smile tightened into something she hoped didn't look like a grimace. "Cameron died."

Pablo didn't reveal a flicker of concern. This matter was a show to him—something seen from behind a lens. But to her, it was the culmination of a decade's work on her business. If the contest continued tomorrow, when the rumours would continue flying thick and fast about her role in Cameron's death, there was no way she'd win.

"Cameron would want us to go on," Leah said, surprising Jessica with the strength of her voice as she stepped closer to the camera. The young woman's chestnut hair flowed in artful waves, and her tear-stained cheeks looked fresh and dewy. "He knew how important this competition was, and he'd want us to continue."

"That's exactly what we think. Cameron wouldn't want anything to change." Pablo ran a hand through his tousled hair and winked. "Though, in fact, there is one change on the cards. It's only fair to warn you now, as I don't think anyone needs more surprises. There's a twist on the format tomorrow. The head-to-head bake isn't just for points. It's an elimination round. Whoever loses tomorrow's bake is out of the contest."

17

Before Jessica had chance to say anything more, Leah raced back to her truck to practise. Jessica still couldn't believe the contest was going to continue. Tomorrow, she'd be expected to smile and make small talk about flavours and decorations, but a murder accusation was hanging over her head. How could she keep going? More than that, how could she possibly win?

She was standing on the opposite side of the village square to Verse View. In front of her, Resolution Road glowed with the late-summer sun, which lit the sandstone flags like they were flecked with gold. The cottage-lined street was made more entrancing by the hanging baskets and planters that bloomed with pansies, petunias, begonias, fuchsias, and geraniums in the bold colours of a child's paintbox. The sight held such a simple, honest beauty that Jessica couldn't believe she was only two minutes from the grisly murder scene she'd found that morning.

Her head swirled with the impossibility of it all. How could she return to her truck and make cakes?

She looked across the square to Verse View. Over there, the promise of Pippa—the spirit-lifting yeast to her dough—called. The shopkeeper had been her best friend since birth, and Jessica was sorely tempted to hide away with her like a little kid, back when blanket forts and tight hugs were places of escape.

But she couldn't do that. There was someone else she needed to speak to instead. She dialled Olympia Fitzherbert, a woman from the baking show's production company whose job title contained words like "executive" and "coordinator" that really didn't explain her role but made clear her significance.

"First, let me say how terribly sorry we all are about the events of the day." Olympia had a voice for radio. It was strong but soothing, and something about it sounded familiar from the very first word. "It's awful what you've been through, and we're all here to support whatever you need."

Before Jessica could explain that what she needed was to pause the production schedule, Olympia continued.

"I've already personally spoken with members of Cameron's family, and we'll be liaising with them throughout this difficult process."

Jessica bit back her comment on the idea of *liaising* with a grieving family. Olympia's voice was pleasant enough, but the woman herself was all business. It wasn't entirely surprising she didn't talk about *comforting* Cameron's relatives. "How are his family?"

Jessica couldn't imagine Cameron's parents or siblings. He was in his early thirties, like her, so she assumed he had plenty of living relatives. But he hadn't mentioned them once. In fact, he hadn't spoken about anyone outside of the contest. His existence seemed as bleak as the windswept moors at the edge of Little Quillington. As though called by the thought of the wild environment, a breeze tugged several curls free from Jessica's ponytail and whipped them across her face.

"Doing as well as can be expected. I'll let them know you were asking."

"Thank you." Olympia would do no such thing, Jessica was sure.

She walked along the cobbles of Resolution Road and crouched next to a pot of neon-bright fuchsias. Bees danced drunkenly around them, and a group of sparrows hopped along the kerb nearby, taking no notice of Jessica. Olympia sounded as preoccupied as the birds—someone spoke to her on the other end of the call, and she erupted in a flurry of typing.

"And do they..." Jessica wasn't sure how to ask this question, but she couldn't let the opportunity slip away. "Do they have any idea who might have done this to him?"

"Do who have what?" Olympia asked.

"Do his family know who—"

"Yes, I'll be there in a moment," Olympia snapped in her muffled voice. "Apologies. I'm sure you can understand the commotion this terrible news has caused. But it's actually great that you've called. I was wanting to let you know how glad we all are that everything's going ahead tomorrow. Pablo just called in an update, and I told him I wasn't a bit surprised—you've always been a team player."

"Actually..." She took a deep breath. "I'm wondering if we can push back the head-to-head. Leah's really quite upset, and—"

"Your care for other bakers is exactly what the public values about you. Numbers are coming in very strong on that." A tapping sound arose at the other end of the phone. "However, one place where the numbers aren't looking nearly so rosy is overall viewership. We've had word from higher up that we absolutely have to increase the must-see value. We need eyeballs on us every week, and we're being told we've really got to up the tension."

"More tension?" Jessica clutched her free hand to the flowerpot to keep from tumbling back at this news. "One of the contestants has just died. Isn't that enough?"

"You're thinking on the right lines." Olympia's voice was as bright and bold as the sun that beat onto Jessica's head. Did the woman really think it was good that Cameron had died? "The bosses acknowledge that the publicity from that is a positive."

"That's not what I meant." This conversation was getting so far away from Jessica she could barely follow it. She felt the same helplessness as the first time she'd tried to make caramel and watched the sugar burn in an instant.

"Cameron always was the bad boy of baking—the contestant that viewers loved to hate. His demise should give everyone a feeling of closure over his exit from the contest. And it'll keep attention on the show."

"But he—"

"And of course"—Olympia's voice sharpened, and the sunny scene around Jessica dropped away—"there's further tension from your involvement in his death. I'm hearing rumours from my news contacts that you're in the frame for this."

"What? No, I didn't do it. I—"

"Everyone here's entirely behind you, Jessica, I hope you know. Full support and all that."

"I didn't kill Cameron."

"Like I said, we're with you all the way. And while you're on the show, it's my job to manage the press around you. I'm currently pushing back very hard on tomorrow's front pages, which are lurid, to say the least." Olympia fell silent for a moment to let her meaning sink in. Then, apparently to ensure her point hit home, she added, "Should you need to delay or even step away from the contest, however, I would, with deep regret, be forced to withdraw my efforts."

Jessica had been on the show long enough to translate that TV speak into English. If she didn't go ahead with tomorrow's contest, Olympia would stop managing the baying hounds in the press. She'd let them destroy Jessica's life in an instant.

18

Jessica buried her head in her hands. She'd entered this contest to change her life, and as she twined her fingers through her corkscrew curls, she reminded herself to be careful what she wished for.

Pressing clammy fingers against her eyes, she pictured the cover stories of tomorrow's newspapers. Her spinning mind served up headlines before she could stop it:

Kitchen Nightmare Turns Deadly: Baker Charged with Murder

Great British Breakdown: Baker Linked to Killing

Contestant Kneads to Explain: Deadly Mix-Up in Street Bakes Showdown

It wouldn't matter that the police hadn't even interviewed her. Right then, she was enough of a suspect to justify column inches, if not feet. Olympia had said she was doing her best to manage the press, but she could only do so much. In fact, knowing her need for more tension around the show, she *would* do only so much to help. A suggestion that one of the show's bakers had killed another was great for ratings. This situation was just what Olympia needed. Jessica only hoped the slick woman would keep journalists from whipping up a full-force hate campaign. The British press were alarmingly talented at doing that, and Jessica would never recover.

She recalled her first experience with the attention the show had brought her. She'd been in the contest barely a week before her entire Askew backstory came out and the media labelled her the rogue ingredient in a beloved family recipe.

Perhaps she'd been naïve not to expect that, but she hadn't thought a baking competition would attract such press. It probably wouldn't have if people like Cameron hadn't been selected from the applicant pool for the drama. As Jessica thought this, it hit her that she, too, might have been chosen for that reason. Her contentious family history brought attention that a new TV show sorely needed.

Back then, the headlines about her black-sheep status were hurtful, and the quotes from Aunt Enriqueta and the others who agreed with her about Jessica's *betrayal of the Askew legacy* were even worse. During the early weeks of the contest, she'd considered dropping out.

Now, she'd click her heels with happiness if gossip about her family was the worst thing she was facing.

Instead, she was hunched over a flowerpot, fingers pressed to her eyes to keep tears from leaking out, wondering just how bad the murder accusations might be.

How had she got here?

Jessica forced the image of herself on the front page out of her brain. But as she did this, another picture took its place. It was her food truck, the Rolling Pin, with its distinctive bright-pink decoration and rainbow sprinkles. *The Great British Street Bakes Showdown* wasn't just about individuals. It focused on the food trucks too. When she'd entered the show, Jessica had been excited for the recognition that element would bring her business.

Now, the truck would be recognisable for all the wrong reasons. When people saw its gorgeous glittery paintwork, they wouldn't think of cookies and cupcakes. Their minds would go straight to murder.

How could she fix this? Her fingers itched to pull out her phone and call a journalist so she could explain that this was all a terrible mistake. But who would listen to her protestations of innocence? Nobody. Nothing would replace her in the papers until the real murderer was found.

Jessica stared down at the centuries-old cobbles beneath her feet. These stones had a solidity and sureness she sorely needed.

She had to find out who'd killed Cameron. And quickly. Her determination was as strong as a rolling pin. But she had no idea where to start. The production company was no help, she had no way to get in touch with the dead baker's family, and her only real suspect was a tiny, lovestruck young woman who surely hadn't got the strength to bring down the "tattooed bad boy of baking." Jessica didn't have a clue who might have killed Cameron. But if she didn't find someone soon, the finger of suspicion would stay firmly pointed at her.

She took out her phone and typed messages to the two people she was close to on the show. She'd gone into the competition assuming it would be like *The Great British Bake Off*, where contestants helped and hugged one another through every mistake. But food-truck people were a different breed. They'd chosen life on wheels for a reason. She'd hung out with only a couple of her competitors outside of filming, and even then, she wouldn't call them friends.

Ideally, they were close enough that they'd share what they knew about Cameron. Really, though, what could that be? His bad temper had kept everyone at arm's length after his initial charm offensive failed. Leah claimed that even the bad temper was faked. Was there any chance Jessica would find enough truth about him to be led to the killer?

She didn't know, but it was her only shot at clearing the suspicion that was focused squarely on herself. She stared at her phone and willed a reply to come through.

But then she heard a sharp yell nearby, and she forgot about her phone entirely.

19

"No! Absolutely not! You can't film here! Take that camera out of my face!"

At the sound of this bellow, Jessica stood so quickly that her head spun. She leaned against a sun-warmed cottage wall as purple spots danced before her eyes, and she looked around for the camera someone was shouting about.

But she couldn't see even the glint of a hidden lens.

"Out! Out!"

Jessica grasped that the voice—and the camera—were back in the village square. And when she realised who the shouting person was, she raced back there to prevent a second killing that day.

She covered the few feet along Resolution Road in a record dash then turned left and ran straight to Mrs Merdle's Miscellany. Outside the shop, Mrs Merdle was brandishing the enormous rolling pin she kept solely for this purpose.

"It'll be great publicity for your shop," Pablo said, backing away from Mrs Merdle's weapon and the pink-fleshed, well-fed arm that wielded it. "Perhaps you didn't understand. We're a *national* show."

Mrs Merdle's nostrils flared, and her beady eyes glinted. Pablo was dangerously close to finding out the surprising strength of this five-foot-nothing shopkeeper.

"Sorry!" Jessica cried, leaping in front of Pablo and stretching her arms wide like a shield. "What he meant to say was he's sorry for bothering you." Jessica swallowed hard and held her ground. "And can *I* say what a fetching apron you're wearing today? The pattern really is quite... dazzling."

Mrs Merdle didn't smile—rumour had it she'd smiled only once in her entire life, on the day her no-good husband died—but she did lower her rolling pin. She slipped it into the pocket of her wraparound 1940s-style apron and clamped her chapped red hands on her hips. "You tell that filming lad he's not to be bothering me."

The woman glared at Jessica—or perhaps glared through her to Pablo—for several long seconds. The tension in the air was as thick as buttercream. Then she stomped back to her shop and slammed the door behind her. Jessica breathed a sigh of relief. The last thing she needed was to get on the wrong side of Mrs Merdle.

She'd felt scared enough of the woman that morning, when she'd taken Pippa's hidden supplies of butter. Mrs Merdle had made her scones with margarine instead, thanks to Jessica, who shivered at the thought of even that being discovered. She wouldn't give Mrs Merdle any further reason to oppose her.

Though the shopkeeper looked like a fishwife at home with a tub and dolly on washday, she was in fact the richest woman in all of Little Quillington. Nobody knew where she kept her money, but she had plenty of it. She owned at least half the local buildings and doled out high-interest loans to those desperate enough to risk retribution from her rolling pin.

She was almost as powerful as the Askew family, and she certainly didn't need publicity from Pablo.

Jessica took several deep breaths to calm her body after its latest flood of adrenaline. She should have been used to this sort of scenario—food trucks brought short, sharp bursts of business and quick turnarounds. Her time on the baking show had taken those experiences to another level. She'd spent the past weeks in a state of barely suppressed panic, coping with one challenge after another. Her head was filled with an up-to-the-minute points tally—both her own and her competitors'—as well as feedback from each episode on social media. She was constantly adjusting her ideas, making sure she aimed high enough to stay near the top of the rankings without taking a risk that might mean eviction. She'd been living on a knife-edge, always ready to spring into action.

But now, she was dealing with the clash of the baking show, the life she'd once run away from, and the killing she'd stumbled onto that morning, and she wondered what past Jessica had ever been worried about.

As she turned to face Pablo, she saw that dark shadows of stress ringed his eyes. But his gaze also held a spark of defiance.

"That woman seriously overreacted." He puffed up his skinny chest, as though he hadn't been hiding behind Jessica a moment ago.

"Mrs Merdle's entitled to her privacy." Jessica never would have thought she'd defend the woman who'd once yanked her into the square by the ear and announced that Jessica had said a curse word in her shop. "She's got nothing to do with the contest, so why were you filming her? I was told this hometown visit would involve a couple of interviews with close friends and family and some shots of the place I grew up in. Mrs Merdle shouldn't be involved with this."

Pablo pulled a folded scrap of paper from his pocket. "Apparently she owns the buildings that back onto"—he glanced down—"Index Alley, where you found Cameron's body. I was filming an interview about that. Trying to, anyway."

Jessica pictured the brightly decorated cakes and cutely animated food trucks of the baking show's credits. At no point after seeing them would viewers expect an interview about a crime scene.

Pablo fiddled with one of the hoops in his ear. Then he muttered, "That violent response of hers was totally unwarranted. I thought provincial types were meant to be welcoming."

Biting back her reply to that typical London attitude, she focused on the piece of paper in Pablo's hand. "How did you find out she owns those buildings?"

He shrugged but couldn't quite conceal the pride beneath his cool-guy façade. "Gigs like this baking lark just pay the rent. I'm actually a documentary maker. I'm all about exposing the truth *they* don't want you to know." His wide eyes and jerk of the chin on the word "they" made Jessica flinch. "Getting information from people is my job. It didn't take long to find this out. Thought she'd be more willing to get on film, though. Most business owners are. Sensible ones, anyway."

Jessica looked over Pablo's shoulder at his ever-present film crew, who she'd almost forgotten were there. As always, they'd seen everything. She hoped they didn't actually use what they'd seen of Mrs Merdle, or they'd learn the true might of the small but shrewd woman.

Then Jessica's thought repeated: *they'd seen everything.*

The film crew, who'd been here all day, had seen everything. They'd been filming in the square that morning, mere metres from where Cameron was killed. Jessica's heart spun up to full speed again—quicker even than her beloved KitchenAid—as fresh adrenaline whipped through her veins.

She clenched her teeth to keep from saying anything. Not only had Pablo's crew seen everything, he also *knew* that they had. They'd got vital evidence, and Pablo's sharp self-interest surely hadn't allowed him to hand over his only copy to the police. But instead of hooking up the camera to a monitor and poring over the morning's tape, Pablo was out here, doing more filming.

The tingle in her spine told her to be careful. She knew Pablo wasn't the killer—he'd been in her sights while Cameron was being murdered. But Pablo's actions that day made Jessica very wary.

There was danger in Little Quillington, and Jessica had no idea if she was safe. The only thing she could rely on right then was her instincts. She paid attention to the tingle that travelled up her neck and swirled around her skull, telling her to get away.

She would watch that footage somehow. But right now, her body was screaming to get somewhere safe.

20

Keeping her head down to avoid the glare she knew Mrs Merdle would be giving through her window, Jessica walked out of the square and headed down Inkwell Lane, straight to her pink glittery food truck.

It was her home. She didn't sleep in it, but where she laid her head was unimportant. What she cared about were her neat row of chopping knives, her perfectly pliable spatula, and the mixing bowl that fit into the crook of her elbow just so.

She raced back to her truck like a bat to its cave—without any intention beyond hiding away and feeling safe. But as she reached the door, she found something even better awaiting. There, on the hook that usually held her menu, hung a tote bag. *Her* tote bag. A screenprint of Julia Child was smiling beneath the words *Bon appétit*, and after Jessica reached for it, she thrilled at the touch of the sharp-edged butter blocks inside. The butter was cold once more, and when she looked into the bag, she spotted several ice packs nestled among it. She was so happy that tears sprang to her eyes.

This bag could have been put here only by Pippa, who was now more than ever the chocolate chips to her cookie. The rainbow-coloured ice packs alone were a giveaway. And as Jessica hooked the tote bag over her shoulder, she remembered where she'd had it last—right outside Pippa's shop.

She tried to push aside the vision that came hot on the heels of this memory, the one that followed a trail of blood towards tragedy. But the image of Cameron lying dead on the

AND THEN THERE WERE SCONES 77

ground wouldn't disappear, no matter how hard she rubbed her eyes.

Only one thing would clear her jumbled head. It was what she'd abandoned her family legacy to pursue, something she'd make any further sacrifice for if needed: baking.

She set the butter on the counter of her food truck and started unwrapping the first golden block. Its surface was cool and smooth, and she traced it with a reverence that most people would never understand.

Some people's fingers were made for stroking velvet and lace. Some longed to delve into tumbling tubs of seeds and beads. Her family's fingers wanted only paper—the smooth matte trace of it touched by ink that turned the world's confusion into neatly contained narratives.

Jessica's fingers, however, had always sought something different. They loved the eager give of risen dough, the sticky dribble of fresh raspberry coulis, and the silken lightness of well-whipped cream. Growing up, she'd tried to pretend at a passion for paper by poring over recipes. Each birthday brought gifts of Mrs Beaton, Nigella Lawson, and Yotam Ottolenghi. But those were never enough.

The words themselves were food for her family. But to Jessica, the *splashes*, *pinches* and *sprinkles* only became real when mixed together—when baked, assembled, and decorated. Every time she'd devoured her own concoctions, the black-and-white world of her upbringing turned Technicolor. Life became real in a way no story every could.

That afternoon, while she was alone in her food truck, her worries melted as easily as butter, and she focused her very essence on the recipe she was making. It was one that would compete head-to-head with Leah's bake the following day, a Yorkshire barm brack.

This recipe had been assigned by the producers of the contest, who must have picked it for the local name. The southerners who made this show had surely never tried the old-fashioned food item. The Yorkshire barm brack was a heavy, fruity tea loaf that made Jessica think of the lace curtains, glass ornaments, and darkened parlours of elderly relatives. It wasn't the sort of indulgent bake that usually sold well from food trucks.

She'd suggested fat rascals instead, fluffy, comforting rock cakes with dried fruit in. But the producers had objected to the name, and when she'd said it also went by "fat scallywag" and "fat scoundrel," they'd claimed she was being purposely obtuse. She'd reluctantly agreed to make barm brack instead.

In many regions, this type of bread was light and airy. In Ireland, it was eaten at new-year celebrations, and it was such a cultural touchstone that it was mentioned in James Joyce's *Dubliners* and sung about by Van Morrison. But the version from Jessica's part of the world was a firm, dense thing that would inspire neither song nor story.

The recipe was simple and perfect for the busy farm- and fisher-folk of Yorkshire, who knew how to make the best of lean times. Most significantly, the recipe didn't include any butter.

Jessica's desperation for the ingredient earlier was because she'd planned to make the ordinary little Yorkshire barm brack into something spectacular. Thanks to Pippa, she'd regained her supply and was back on track.

She stirred the butter into a lemon curd packed with flavour, which would sneak in the richness this dish was missing. Folding vanilla buttercream into the curd made it pipeable, and she created a cupcake-style swirl on top of individual helpings of barm brack. Originally, she'd planned to drizzle a salted honey caramel sauce over the dish to give it a deep note of luxury. But she hadn't picked up any honey that morning, and she couldn't face returning to the busy shops to buy any. Instead, she chose an ingredient closer to her heart and far more available. After plucking rosemary directly from the food truck's window boxes, she roasted enough leaves to make a sweet, surprising jelly. The flavour reminded her of her grandma, who always smelled of the velvety herb.

Dotting the white-and-yellow topping with pretty pearls of glistening jelly made Jessica's cakes look absolutely irresistible.

But this version was only the first. Jessica worked all afternoon, testing out variations of the simple currant-packed cake base and its flavourful toppings. She candied lemon peel, but the texture was too chewy. Then she shredded the rind, made a zingy marmalade, and added a surprising core to the cake. This result was far better but made a single bite feel overwhelming. Playing with sizes and proportions took up the remainder of the afternoon, and as her shoulders started to seize from too much whipping, she was finally forced to rest.

When she looked at the clock, she realised her break had come just in time—the day had disappeared! She'd planned to meet Pippa in the nearby Quill and Well at eight, and she had only a few minutes spare to wash the flour from her face and shake a little life back into her curls before leaving.

As she stepped into the last golden light of the evening, she glanced at her phone. She'd avoided it all day, knowing from plenty of experience that a watched pot never boiled. Surely, she'd ignored her phone long enough that someone would have replied to her messages about Cameron. Cheery bubbles of notifications on her screen said people had, and her heart soared as she peered at the replies. But it dropped down just as swiftly when she read them. The contestants she'd reached out to didn't know any more about Cameron than she did. As she strode over sun-warmed paving stones, she thought about how strange that was. Even though the show's bakers weren't close, they'd still learned a little about one another between takes. She could recall at least the name of a partner or pet for everyone else she'd competed against in the past few weeks. But not for Cameron.

When it came to him, she knew nothing. She scoured her mind more vigorously as she turned onto the square. Had he even said where he was from? She'd assumed London from his accent, but that was easy enough to fake. As she pictured him, she saw the neat black lines of dozens of tattoos. Had he ever shared stories about them? None that she could recall. Though she could guess the meaning behind one of them. On the ring finger of his left hand, he had the thin circle of an inked-on wedding band. He had other rings tattooed on as well, but those looked so dark they had to be brand new. Perhaps they were to distract from the one he'd got first.

Had Cameron been married? Any ex-wife of his would surely have a motive, given what Jessica knew of him. If she could find the woman, that would be an excellent lead.

But that would have to wait just a little longer. She'd promised Pippa some cakes, and after her exhausting day, she needed a little rest before beginning the search for Cameron's killer.

Pippa was already waiting, and her older sister, Madeline, was sitting by her at a corner table. Jessica's heart warmed at the sight of the oldest Pankhurst sibling, whose laughter was the sugar that would sweeten any day. She and Madeline had waved across the square that morning, but Jessica had been too busy to stop. If only she had, she realised, this entire day would have gone differently. Somebody else would have found Cameron's body, and she wouldn't be so very tangled up in the situation that now threatened to ruin her life. Though perhaps that was wishful thinking. Her baking-show rival had died in her hometown, and even she struggled to believe there wasn't a connection.

At least she had the prospect of a drink with Pippa and Madeline to brighten the end of the difficult day. If anyone could make her feel better, that pair could. Madeline was a vicar, but she had come to the ministry late and saw religious work as no reason to change her fun-loving attitude. Although utterly dedicated to her calling, she still managed to fill life with more mischief than the fictional French schoolgirl she was named for. Her company was just what was needed to relieve the dark shadow that hung over the day.

But as Jessica saw the look on Madeline's face, she realised the rest and reprieve she so sorely craved were not on the cards that evening.

21

"I'm going to need a drink for this, aren't I?" Jessica asked, handing her cake boxes over to Pippa and Madeline and then going to buy a round of pints.

The local brewery changed its offerings regularly, so she enjoyed a moment of respite while choosing between those currently on tap. Beer and Loathing in Las Vegas didn't appeal. However, An Ale of Two Cities and The Handmaid's Ale both sounded inviting. Because of the way her day was going so far, she opted for the strongest one.

She sat down and took a swig of her Margaret-Atwood–inspired beverage before meeting Madeline's anxious gaze.

"You know I would never reveal anything a parishioner tells me in confidence," Madeline started, wiping away froth traces left by her own long swallow. "However, my position does afford me opportunities to interact with a wide range of people, including those more naturally inclined to disclose updates on community news."

Pippa rolled her eyes. "We get it. Church ladies love to gossip, but you personally are a saint who's above such things."

Madeline elbowed her sister in the ribs. The older Pankhurst couldn't be described as saintly, and in fact, it was easy to forget she was a vicar when she was out of uniform. But since joining the ministry, Madeline had certainly taken her spiritual duties seriously. "I just want to make it clear that I wouldn't tell Jessica what I'm about to unless the information was openly shared and I really thought it important she know."

Jessica tipped back her pint glass again, wanting the numbness it contained to protect her from whatever was coming. She rarely drank—her job's early mornings meant she prioritised good sleep and a clear head. But a day like this called for a libation. "I'm ready. What have people been saying about me? That I'm a killer?" She'd thought hearing herself say the word might take the edge off. But her heart skipped a beat as she spoke it aloud.

Madeline shook her head. "It's not about that...Well, it is, but it's more complicated, and—"

It was Pippa's turn to nudge her sister sharply. "Is there a point on the way?"

"Yes." Madeline opened one of the cake containers before her. Instead of reaching in for a taste, she simply breathed deeply. The calm that washed over her face was the reason Jessica loved baking. "Our flower ladies were in the church this evening, bringing back unsold items from the white elephant stall at the fête."

"Flower ladies?" Jessica asked. The church in Little Quillington famously had no flower arrangements. Its displays were origami created from old book pages.

Madeline grimaced. "Sorry, I shouldn't call them that. I mean Petunia, Iris, Daisy and Violet. They're a wonderful asset to the church. They run the food drive at Harvest Festival, make pomanders and Christingles with the kids at Christmas, and hide eggs for the hunt at Easter."

"It sounds like they're very involved in the community." Jessica didn't know all these women, but she was fairly certain Iris was a nurse and Petunia ran the choir. Both would be described as busybodies by someone less tactful than Madeline.

The vicar's crooked smile confirmed what Jessica said. "While they were at the church this afternoon, they joined me for a cup of tea. They mentioned that..." Madeline leaned down for another long inhalation of the cake. The sweet lemon tang that filled the air seemed to give her strength to continue. "They mentioned that your aunt Enriqueta has been speaking with the rest of the Askews a great deal today. Apparently, they've been discussing this morning's events quite... energetically."

Jessica swallowed hard. "I assumed that would be the case. Has she been saying I'm a killer?" Again, the word sent a sparkle of shock through her whole body.

"It's a little more than that, I'm afraid. She's using the situation to... Well, I don't quite know how to put this delicately." Madeline took a decidedly un-vicarly swig. "She's trying to get your grandma removed from the Askew board."

Jessica shook her head, as if she could shake some sense into those words. "From the board? What? Why? And how is that related to this morning? Has something happened to my grandma?"

Then Jessica's heart froze, refusing to beat at this thought. Her eyes welled with tears so quickly that Madeline sprang forwards and clutched her shoulder.

"No, I'm sorry. I'm not explaining this at all." The vicar's brow furrowed deeply. "It's just... I don't really know how to say it."

"Mads!" Pippa's voice was stern. "You're scaring us. What's going on?"

Pippa was right. Madeline, whose job involved comforting those in the worst times of distress, was usually a source of calm and peace. Right now, she was anything but.

"In the Askew family, each shop owner has a seat on the board," Madeline said, speaking with a slow composure that was clearly a struggle. "Your grandma has one, and when she one day... passes over, the seat will go, along with her shop, to her heir."

Jessica nodded, blinking back fresh tears. She'd lost her parents young and been raised by her grandma. It was impossible to think about losing her too.

"You're her heir," Madeline said. The words seeped like syrup into Jessica's brain, but instead of explaining anything, they merely glued up the mechanisms that turned ideas into understanding.

"Your aunt is saying that now you're tied up in a murder investigation, you're doing irreparable harm to the family. She's questioning your grandma's judgement because of her closeness with you, and she's convinced the rest of the family that if you inherit her board seat, you'll destroy the Askew legacy. I'm so sorry. This must be difficult to hear." She squeezed Jessica's shoulder once more and looked her in the eye before continuing. "But you should know what's happening. Your aunt is convening the board tomorrow evening as soon as the shops close. They'll vote then on removing your grandma's seat."

Jessica couldn't entirely make sense of the words that rang in her ears. Could her aunt even do that? Jessica's heart tore at the thought of it.

"My grandma's done everything for this family." Her voice was softer than sifted flour. But inside her mind was a wild kettle-steam scream.

22

"I have to... I need to..." Jessica finished her beer with a sense of determination, and her legs tensed to stand. But where could she go?

Pippa put a fresh drink in her hands. "You need to make a plan."

She took a large swig, as though fuelling up for action, but what could she really do? Jessica slumped back in her seat. "How? With my grandma away, Aunt Enriqueta has the biggest influence over the family. People are too scared to go against her, and they certainly won't listen to me."

"So we just need your grandma back here!" Pippa slammed her glass down a little too forcefully, and beer sloshed onto the table.

"She's delivering a book to the royal family tomorrow. There's a big celebration at the Palace, and she won't be back here until Monday." As she helped Pippa wipe up the spill, Jessica thought about what her aunt's actions meant. "But she will be back, and she'll be angry about this. So why is Aunt Enriqueta doing it? To her own mother? She can't hope to get away with it in the long run. The consequences will be..."

Madeline's face softened into the expression of tender comfort Jessica had expected earlier. "I'm sorry to tell you this, but your grandma's not been very well lately."

The jagged tear in Jessica's heart widened. "Really? No. I would have known."

She looked at Pippa, who was glaring at her sister. "She didn't want you to find out."

With a small nod, Madeline agreed. "She didn't want to worry you during the contest. She was so excited for you, and she asked people not to tell you."

Pippa reached across the table and stroked Jessica's hand.

"But she..." Jessica recalled the dozens of photos from her grandma in recent weeks, each one showing off a different dress-and-hat combination. The kind old woman had been so excited to choose just the right outfit for her trip to the Palace. If she was ill enough that Aunt Enriqueta was ready to take a stand against her, this could be Grandma's last chance to have such a special day. Jessica wasn't letting anyone take that from the woman who'd raised her, no matter what. "I have to stop this."

She tipped up her glass and was surprised to find it empty. But before she could order another round, Madeline dashed to the bar and came back bearing crisp, fizzy ginger beers, explaining that "the smell of your cakes made me crave this."

"Ginger syrup," Jessica whispered to herself, her nose tingling as she realised that was the final ingredient needed to perfect her Yorkshire barm brack. She could drizzle the syrup on before adding the topping, and the flavours would combine into something far greater than the sum of their parts. If only the confusing mess of events in her life could be tied up so neatly.

Pippa and Madeline ate the cakes Jessica had made that day and drank in silence.

Jessica chewed her fruit-rich tea loaf slowly, appreciating the firm spring of the sponge, which was moist and delicious despite containing no butter. The bright zing of lemon in the topping made her thoughts race. "I should have seen this coming from my aunt."

"She is pretty evil," Pippa mumbled through a mouthful of cake. Then she dodged another elbow in the ribs from her sister. "Sorry, I mean morally challenged."

"No arguments here." Jessica licked rosemary jelly from her fingers. "But this actually makes perfect sense. The shops on Askew Avenue are owned by a family trust. The right to run one is granted by the board, and they usually abide by each person's inheritance wishes. But they have the final say."

"And your aunt has three children," Pippa said, stroking an imaginary goatee and leaning forwards.

That was true. The oldest, Beatrix, had inherited a property from a distant cousin and set up a graphic novel shop at the end of Askew Avenue in the only location without a direct descendent in line. The middle child, Aldous, would take over Criminally Good Mysteries one day. But Dante, who was only two days older than Jessica, was due nothing. For ambitious Aunt Enriqueta, that would never do. Removing Jessica's grandma's board seat was the perfect way to control who inherited her coveted shop in the middle of Askew Avenue.

Pippa swallowed hard. "We need to speak to the board members."

"Or clear my name in Cameron's murder," Jessica said. "That would give Aunt Enriqueta far less ammunition. But at this point, neither option seems possible."

"Oh!" Pippa reached into her pocket, grabbed her phone, and pulled up a website. "I totally forgot. Hattie was in the shop earlier, and she showed me this forum where fans discuss the baking contest."

"Is this a new crack on your screen?" Jessica squinted at it, while Pippa ignored her question about what was sure to be yet another Hattie disaster.

"Just look! There are lots of theories here."

"I can see my name, if that's what you're pointing to." Jessica had visited this forum before, when she first joined the show, and instantly regretted it. The fans on here were rabid, and they made the sort of comments that stuck like molten sugar to bare skin.

"No, hang on, scroll down.... Here! There's a link to the only interview Cameron gave while he was on the show. Well, it looks more like someone shoved a camera in his face while he was at a bar, but he does talk about a few personal things. The connection's not great in here. I'll send you the link, but the key bit is when he talks about being selected for the contest. The person asking him questions is talking about *Love Island*, which had a great season this year. I know you won't have seen it because you've been busy, but I have to catch you up on—"

"Pip." Madeline tapped her fingers against her glass. "Your train of thought is dangerously close to jumping the tracks."

"Right. Anyway, the person who shoves the camera in Cameron's face is talking about *Love Island* and how the show's stars are all picked from social media, and they're not really regular people looking for love. Which, of course, yeah, we all know. And he asks Cameron if it's the same on the baking programme. Did people really apply or were they approached by the production company because of their big online followings?"

Jessica had wondered something similar. Cameron's bad temper seemed a little too perfect for grabbing headlines, much like Jessica's famous family history. "What did he say?"

"The recording isn't very clear. I've listened several times, but he gets angry at this point and walks away. The camera follows him, and it sounds like he says he didn't get on the show using either of those tactics." Pippa's voice lowered as she leaned even closer to Jessica. "Cameron says someone on the inside got him in."

23

Jessica's head reeled from this strange revelation. She switched back from ginger beer to the strong stuff for her next drink, which she then sipped while trying to understand what Cameron meant.

Someone had got him onto the show. She'd applied via the contest's website, following a link in an ad targeting food-truck owners. She hadn't asked the other competitors how they'd got their places, but she'd assumed they'd all gone about it the same way.

If Cameron had got around this process, that made his death even more complicated. He'd somehow snuck onto the show that had taken up the last few weeks of his life. But whoever had got him on hadn't managed to win him special favours when he was there. Cameron had had the same types of disasters as the rest of them—in the week that Jessica's foolproof sponge fell, his buttercream split without reason. He'd blamed others for his mistakes, but everyone seemed to fumble under the pressure of the cameras. Then again, someone had apparently been fired for swapping his sugar and salt the week before. What could this mean?

Jessica's head spun with the twist Pippa's news put on her understanding of the show's past few weeks. Or perhaps it was the beer she'd been drinking more rapidly than intended that was turning her thoughts into a jumbled mess.

"How can we help?" Madeline asked.

Jessica looked in Madeline's warm and earnest eyes and had no idea what to say. Everything she learned about Cameron made his death more confusing. There was no way for Jessica to solve it and clear her name quickly enough to help her grandma. The board were going to vote her out for her association with a suspected killer, and there was nothing Jessica could do.

"There has to be some way to stop your aunt." Pippa drummed her purple-tipped nails on the table. "Could we stop the board meeting or lodge an objection with them?"

Jessica shrugged weakly. "I don't know much about how that all works. I've been away, and I just... I barely know anything about the family business, really. It looks small and quaint, but the large Askew empire goes back centuries, and there's a whole book of bylaws I've never even looked at."

Pippa's nails drummed faster. "Your family's big! That's got to be helpful. I think the objection thing could work. The board can't remove someone if the rest of the family supports them. And your grandma is lovely; we must be able to drum up support. Maybe not among the shop owners here that your aunt's scared into submission. But there are tonnes of you. Wherever books can be found, there's an Askew lurking nearby."

Jessica opened her mouth to deny that assertion, but it was true. Only those in the main family line inherited the precious shops on Askew Avenue, and they were in short supply. The rest of the family found jobs in the highest ranks of the literary world. Her cousins Rudyard and Kipling were shining examples of that pattern. But then she thought about who had found the cousins their positions—Aunt Enriqueta.

She, Pippa, and Madeline discussed as many members of the family as they could recall, and every one of them owed something to the dark, scheming woman. Jessica was annoyed she'd not noticed that sooner, but Aunt Enriqueta had set this situation up perfectly. As Jessica strained her brain to think of any other people, she realised she had one more option.

"What about the Askews in Hay?"

Pippa and Madeline sat up straight. Their eyes widened. They knew exactly who she meant. A breakoff line of the family had moved to Hay-on-Wye, a rival book town in Wales, which was famous for hosting a literary festival each summer. These relatives had set up shops there and thrown their name around to bring in business. The Askews of Little Quillington did not associate with them, which Pippa and Madeline knew all too well.

"I know it's an extreme option."

"To say the least," Madeline murmured.

"But I think they'd help." Jessica focused on the lids of her now-empty cake boxes, fitting them on carefully and sealing them with a firm click. "Don't you?"

Pippa opened her mouth to say something. Then she closed it again and gave the smallest of shrugs. There was no saying what the Askews in Hay would do. Nobody in Little Quillington even mentioned them, or acknowledged the small town they lived in. The rivalry with them went back decades, and suggesting an alliance was only half a step below a deal with the devil.

"My grandma wouldn't like it." Jessica stacked her cake boxes. "She always says they'll take over Little Quillington if given half a chance. But..." She lowered her voice and leaned closer to the sisters. "I did a food festival in Hay last year and met some of them. They seem like perfectly nice people."

Pippa and Madeline's eyes widened even further.

Jessica pushed back her chair. "They're only a couple of hours' drive away. I could go there and bring as many of them as I can back, and—"

"You can't drive now. You've been drinking." Pippa planted her hands on the thickly varnished table, looking ready to leap over it to stop Jessica if needed.

"I've never felt more sober in my life," Jessica replied. "But you're right. I'll eat something more substantial than cake and wait a few hours. I could drive over late tonight and speak with them first thing in the morning. That would give me plenty time to get back before the board meets at eight."

"It's too dangerous."

"I said I'll wait till I'm sober."

"You're exhausted. You shouldn't drive tonight at all. And besides, someone from your baking show has just been killed. How do you know Cameron was their only target? If they're after all the contestants, haring around country roads alone is an easy way to get yourself crossed off their list."

"I just...I need to..." Adrenaline coursed through Jessica, keeping her from even completing her thoughts properly.

"The board isn't meeting until tomorrow evening. We can find a way to fix this in the morning."

Before Jessica could fight back, Madeline leaned closer to her and looked deep into her eyes. "Right now, we're going to get some sleep. All of us. Things will look better in the light of a new day."

Jessica's heartbeat drummed the rhythm of escape. But she knew the sisters were talking sense. It didn't feel that way, but she had known them long enough for their words to hold sway.

They were as trustworthy to her as flour, milk, and eggs. She believed them even over her own rising panic.

"You're staying at your grandma's tonight, right?" Pippa asked, though the question was unnecessary. Jessica's grandma's house was where she'd grown up, and she always stayed there when visiting the village. "We'll stay with you."

Jessica let herself be led through the back entrance to her grandma's shop and up the stairs. Being on Askew Avenue felt strange, but nobody would disturb them here, even while her grandma was away. She was safe.

When she lay down in bed, she found a soft lump between the sheets. It was a bright pink knitted cupcake. Her grandma had made this object and left it as a gift.

Jessica clutched it tightly and fell into a deep and much-needed sleep.

24

When Jessica awoke the next morning, she kept the covers clamped over her head. She knew better than to try leaving the safety of her bed. Her problems were impossible to fix—a murder accusation lingered around her, an unknown killer could be after her next, and because of her, Aunt Enriqueta was pushing her beloved grandma off the Askew family board.

She willed herself to go back to sleep, but her ears soon picked up voices outside her bedroom that were tough to ignore.

"We should wake her."

"She's too stressed right now. Sleep is what her body needs."

The Pankhurst sisters continued this debate long enough for Jessica to give up the idea of dozing off. Against her better judgement, she grabbed her phone from the bedside table.

Among the countless notifications—none of which she wanted to see, since they had to be about her connection to a murder—she spotted one in all caps. The message was from Olympia, the producer she'd spoken with the day before. It reminded her, yet again, that she needed to attend the head-to-head contest that morning or forfeit her place in the competition.

The bright morning light had indeed brought the clarity Madeline had promised. But this wasn't the positive change Jessica had wanted. Instead, it was like a blowtorch setting her hopes to flambé.

Jessica couldn't figure out who'd really killed Cameron. She couldn't drive a carload of distant relatives to shout down her aunt's dastardly plans. In fact, all she'd ever been able to do was bake. The thought of sifting, stirring, slicing, and serving made her anxious chest relax enough for her to breathe.

"You're not going in there," one of the Pankhurst sisters whispered furiously. It was impossible to tell which one it was—when angry, they all sounded alarmingly like their mother.

"It's fine!" Jessica called through the door. "I'm awake, and I'm getting up. Madeline, you need to head to church. If the vicar is late, it's pretty tough for the service to go ahead. Pippa, you need to go to work too. I'm just getting dressed and heading out now. We've all got things to do!"

After fierce hugs and assurances that she really was OK, she raced out the back door and across the village. Then she drove her sparkly pink food truck to the far end of Askew Avenue. Here, with the wild moors at her back and the village square barely visible past the stretch of cobbles, she parked up and started her opening tasks. Glimpses of her family's shops through the windows threatened to fill her head with worries. But she forced herself to concentrate on the checklist she'd used each day for years.

She turned on the oven, tested the mixers, checked the temperature of the fridge, confirmed her ingredients list, and went through the dozen other elements of her opening routine.

By the time her neon pink flamingo clock ticked close to eight, she was ready to bake. She wouldn't actually start work for a couple of hours, but she liked to have everything in place before the film crew began recording. Otherwise, she risked forgetting something simple while baking, thereby adding to the large number of scrunched panic-faces to make it on screen.

AND THEN THERE WERE SCONES 99

She was nearly sure she'd remembered everything. The proximity of her family was so distracting that she couldn't be entirely certain, even though she hadn't yet seen any of them. Their shops were presence enough. Jessica was thankful that Aunt Enriqueta's Criminally Good Mysteries was at the opposite end of the street, and there was little chance that the spiteful woman would come down here on the day she was plotting against Jessica's grandma in the worst possible way.

One other person was conspicuously absent that morning: Leah. The young baker had seemed keen on the contest the day before. But she was nowhere to be seen.

Leah should have been parked beside Jessica, ready to do sound and lighting tests for their head-to-head. But the space on the grass beside her was empty. Perhaps the loss of Cameron had hit her overnight, and she'd deflated like over-proofed dough. Leah seemed to really love the angry young man, and a night without him may have brought the reality of the loss home.

Jessica spotted Pablo walking down Askew Avenue and clearly thinking the same thing. He looked at his watch and frowned. Olympia, from the production team, had said that competitors forfeited if they didn't show up on time.

Excitement rushed through Jessica's chest. She felt bad for Leah, of course, but if the young baker missed today's challenge, Jessica's victory was guaranteed. She would win the whole baking contest and be in with a shot of rescuing her business.

She couldn't think too closely about that. Her truck was linked with murder in people's minds. Coming back from that would be hard. But surely succeeding on the show and earning spots at the top food festivals in the UK would move things in the right direction.

Jessica glanced through her truck's window again. Pablo and his crew were still a good few metres away, and she let herself breathe deeply and linger in one last moment of uncertainty before she slapped on her game face. Then she hopped down to the cobbles and strode over to the crew with a smile.

"Slight hitch!" Pablo called, picking his pace up to a TV-show jog.

"I can see," Jessica said, looking over at the still-empty spot beside her truck. "How's Leah doing?"

"Leah? She's great. She's scoping out alternative locations. We're having a little issue with today's filming permits."

"For this street?" Jessica didn't understand. Her family jumped at any opportunity to show off their businesses on film. Doing so helped them spread the Askew fame far and wide and kept the tourists flowing in. "What's wrong?"

Before he could answer, Jessica spotted a police officer heading towards them. It was Billy, the same moustachioed young man from the day before. He marched along the cobbles like he was on parade.

Jessica's heart pounded. The officer had walked away without asking for so much as a statement yesterday. Had he realised his mistake? Was he coming back now to arrest her? She'd just wanted one more day of baking. Was it really too late?

25

Pablo followed Jessica's gaze to Officer Billy and heaved an exasperated sigh. "Yes, I know. We're moving!" Then he turned back to her. "Your family has apparently revoked their permission to film here, and the police are enforcing their wishes with remarkable speed."

The flames of panic in Jessica's chest calmed—no one was hauling her away to a cell right now. Though the mention of her family kept the fire licking at her heart.

A sharp wind from the moors cut through Pablo's artfully ruffled hair, and he quickly reached up and raked it into place before gesturing to the figure approaching at speed. "I can't even get a meeting with your family about it. They've just sent the youngest police officer known to man to break the news."

The wind brushed the skeletons of last year's leaves onto the street, and it also brought one other, utterly unexpected thing. With bullseye accuracy, a paper airplane bounced against Jessica's left boot and settled at her feet. She looked up. The paper was clean and neatly folded, but she couldn't see who'd thrown it. Other than the film crew, the only person in sight was young Officer Billy.

"I understand there's been a mix-up with the permits today," Jessica said as she bent and pretended to tie her shoe. As she crouched over the airplane, she saw its wings said, "Read me."

"No mix up," Pablo growled, but Jessica waved a hand to silence him as she stood up and skimmed the note. She looked around for the airplane's thrower once more. There was no sign of them, but they'd just given Jessica exactly what she needed.

Billy frowned at Jessica's food truck as he came to a stop with a smart clip of his heels. "As I've already explained, the family has every right to revoke their permission. They own this road, and it's up to them who films here. You're too late for a permit on public land, but you can always try another local business owner with enough parking space to set up in."

The only person who fit that bill was Mrs Merdle, the rolling-pin-wielding woman who Pablo had already offended. She wasn't an option. But Jessica didn't need her anyway, not according to the note on the airplane. She gave young Billy her warmest smile.

"As I said, this is all a misunderstanding," she said before pulling out her driving licence. "*I'm* an Askew. I can grant the permit for filming here myself. Someone else in the family must have thought I'd done that and taken their name off the permit so you'd to come straight to me with any questions."

Pablo's mouth dropped open in surprise, but Billy showed no reaction at all. Clearly, he'd been trained to treat everyone and everything as suspicious, and he was too new to the job to be able to add his own judgement to this situation.

Jessica smiled wider, hoping the rumble of uncertainty in her stomach wasn't audible on the street. She'd never actually used her name to make things happen like this. She didn't know if every Askew could give permission for filming here, but that was what the airplane claimed. She only hoped whoever threw it was on her side. Really, though, what did she have to lose?

Billy's expression was as unchanging as a sauce that refused to thicken. He simply tilted his head towards the radio on his shoulder. "Request to reinstate the filming permit on Askew Avenue." His eyes fixed onto Jessica as he spoke, seeming to expect her to break down and admit she'd lied about her identity. "Application under the name of Jessica Askew." He read some details off the driving licence he still held, and Jessica wondered if giving it to him had been a mistake.

Could she get into trouble by applying for this? Surely not. She really was an Askew. She should have the same rights as the rest of them. But she swallowed hard as he listened to the garbled response from his radio.

Billy straightened, then he folded his hand over Jessica's licence. "They're checking your information."

He said nothing more. But his solid stance told her everything. She couldn't leave. She needed to stay under the watchful eye of the police.

26

Jessica was not good at waiting. She wanted to scurry back to her truck and busy herself with food prep, or hunt for whoever had thrown the paper airplane her way, but taking either action would look like running and hiding to the police officer standing nearby.

Pablo was not a patient person either. He paced around muttering about the light, while the rest of his crew filmed B-roll of the moors that stretched beyond the end of the road.

Billy, by contrast, stood perfectly still, awaiting the next instruction from his radio. He clearly took his job very seriously, but he didn't have an ounce of initiative. Jessica found it odd that he was standing a few streets away from yesterday's murder scene, with an obvious suspect in front of him, and he wasn't asking any questions.

She wouldn't let this opportunity pass her by in the same way.

"I'm glad you're here today, actually," she said. "I wanted to thank you for the calm manner in which you handled yesterday's events."

"Just doing my duty, ma'am," he replied with a sharp nod.

"You shouldn't be so modest." She shot him her widest TV smile. "There aren't many people who could keep their heads while handling a murder. I only spent a few moments down the alley where Cameron died, and it's something I'd never want to see again."

"We're well trained to deal with all manner of situations." His voice was as flat and featureless as a pancake.

"Even murders? I'd hope you don't see too many of them around here."

"Fortunately, not."

Jessica held back a heavy sigh. Talking to this young man was hard work. "The training must really help, though. All I could feel when I saw Cameron was panic. There was so much blood everywhere. I kept thinking someone would leap out and stab me too. He *was* stabbed, wasn't he? I couldn't really see, but there was so much blood, that I thought..."

Finally, a flicker of life appeared in the young officer's eyes. He looked sorely tempted to fill the silence she'd left, and she prayed Pablo didn't walk their way and interrupt.

In a tone more wistful than official, Billy said, "I can't really go into detail about an active investigation."

"Of course not. It's just that I was there, and I'm wondering if I saw something that might help. A dedicated officer like yourself must be eager to solve this high-profile case."

The young man's pale eyes flicked around, checking that nobody was close enough to overhear. He tapped a finger to his temple, which looked like a suggestion that he knew everything. But then he said, "It was a head wound. People are always surprised how much those bleed."

"He hit his head? Could it have been an accident? Did he fall? Slip on something in the alley?" Her questions chased one another eagerly. When she'd found Cameron's blood-soaked body, the scene had been too shocking for her to even consider that he'd simply tripped and landed badly. She'd also been influenced by Cameron's reputation, the twist of guilt in her gut admitted. The bad boy of baking had made plenty of enemies, and it wasn't impossible he'd pushed one of them too far and wound up dead.

"Nope," Billy said, hooking his thumbs into his duty belt and rocking back on his heels. "No chance it was accidental. None at all. The laceration on the side of his head was caused by something with a sharp, solid corner. I suspect it was metal, given the precision of the wound. However, we'll need to wait for forensics to confirm."

"How long will that take?"

"Few days at best. More likely a couple of weeks. It's not as easy as it looks on TV."

Jessica's mind swirled with images of large metal objects. Her food truck was full of them—as was Cameron's—everything from mixers to scales to blenders. But she didn't think any of those items had the sharp corners Billy had described. And it was possible that tests would reveal the weapon to be entirely different from the young officer's guess. If those results weren't back for weeks, though, that wouldn't help.

The mention of TV crime shows made Jessica think of the questions those fictional detectives always asked. "Were there any defensive wounds?"

He shook his head, but before he could add anything, his radio crackled, and he snapped to attention. After a muttered exchange, he beckoned to Pablo.

"The authorisation has come through. Next time, make sure you confirm thoroughly so there aren't any mix-ups. Police time is a valuable commodity."

"It wasn't me who—" Pablo started, but he was cut off by a loud engine pulling up to the end of the street.

AND THEN THERE WERE SCONES 107

A distinctive teal-and-gold food truck parked beside Jessica's, the enormous macaron on its roof wobbling in the wind.

"Finally, we can get started," Pablo said, striding towards the vehicle.

But then Leah stepped out of her truck, and her waxen face, watery eyes, and shaky legs said the day's recording plan was anything but certain.

27

"Are you OK?" Jessica asked, darting to stand between Leah and the camera. There was no way the young baker would want her dishevelled appearance to be caught on film. She was very far from the pink-cheeked, cheery girl who usually drew all eyes to the screen. "We don't have to do this today."

Olympia's insistence that they did indeed have to go ahead rang in Jessica's ears. But Leah looked as though she could barely stand, let alone bake.

Leah took a shuddering breath then pulled her hair into a ponytail. Its usual bouncing chestnut waves hung limply, like squid-ink spaghetti. "Cameron would want us to keep going."

Pablo, who was already setting up the day's shots, clearly had no interest in postponing either. Within moments, the whirlwind of production processes caught up the pair of bakers and sent them through lighting tests, mic-pack set-ups, and camera angle selections. Jessica had been through the routine enough times that she was no longer surprised by the tedium of the time-consuming process. But a frisson of fresh panic still arose when the countdown to filming started, and she pulled on her apron to get ready to bake.

Soon, midmorning arrived, and the shops on Askew Avenue were bustling with customers. None of them came as far as the trucks, but several read the sign nearby saying when food would be served. Jessica heard many excited whispers of the baking contest's name, and those travelled into the bookshops along the street, bringing first her great-uncle's then her cousin's heads to their doors.

Like nervous rabbits at the edges of burrows, these relatives popped their heads out, then in, then out, then in again. News travelled further down the street, and more cousins, aunts, and uncles peeked at Jessica then scurried away.

She expected to see Billy striding back towards her at any moment, ready to revoke her filming permit once word spread that Jessica had tricked him into granting it. But there was no sign of him—or, mercifully, of Aunt Enriqueta. Her shop was at the far end of the street, and Jessica hoped the news slowed to a crawl as it headed her way.

Jessica couldn't worry too much about her aunt then, though. She had cakes to bake. Both she and Leah were making Yorkshire barm bracks, but they were allowed to customise the recipe however they wanted. Jessica had worked on her lemon curd and rosemary jelly topping the day before, and she was adding ginger syrup, thanks to Madeline's innovation. Would those embellishments be enough to win the head-to-head that day?

Jessica and Leah's trucks were parked at an angle, so they could see through just a slice of each other's service hatches. All Jessica had spied so far were the traditional dried currants in jugs of sweet tea used to make the basic recipe. She didn't know what tweaks the young baker had chosen.

She could also see one other significant thing—Leah was looking worse by the minute. When she'd arrived, she'd been unkempt and unsteady. During filming prep, she'd put on a little makeup and had seemed to rally. But as the morning wore on, the clatters and clangs of dropped equipment from her station grew more frequent, and Leah occasionally stopped what she was doing and simply stared into the distance.

Jessica's mind leapt between worry for the young woman and curiosity about what this observation might mean. Was there more to her frazzled state than sorrow? Could a drop of guilt be stirred through it as well? Jessica pushed this curiosity away whenever she caught sight of Leah's darkly shadowed eyes and waxy skin. Whatever was going on, she was struggling.

Before Jessica could think of what to do to help her, Pablo clapped his hands loudly and gathered a crowd of customers.

"You've all seen the show, folks, and now it's your chance to be on it," he said. "It's time for the one-minute warning. Our bakers will be putting out their signs, then you get to run over to whichever truck you choose. Press the pad by each hatch to rate their bakes and send your feedback directly onto the final points tally."

If Jessica hadn't been rushing to pipe neat icing, place cakes into displays, and lean out of the truck hatch to hang the sign explaining her flavours, she'd have stopped and stared in shock at Pablo. She never would have guessed he had such a personable, cheery side.

His voice was starkly contrasted a few moments later by Leah's. As a queue to her truck formed quickly, she shared the tragedy of her loss with everyone who came up for a cake.

She'd added only a rosewater-and-pistachio topping to square slabs of loaf cake—flavours she'd combined often before and which didn't go well with the Yorkshire barm brack base—but the customers at her truck weren't rating her on that choice, apparently. Even before tasting what she'd made, they keyed five stars in on Leah's scoring pad. Five after five after five.

Was she out for the sympathy vote that day? Surely not. That wasn't the point of the competition. But Jessica wondered whether the strained appearance and the tale of woe were an act. If Leah really was that sad, she wouldn't have agreed to baking that day.

The points tally wouldn't be revealed until the televised episode, but Jessica saw enough people giving Leah five stars to be certain that she was ahead.

The public tally counted for only part of the points in this contest. The rest came from the judges, who would receive their servings when Pablo and his team went back to London that evening. But Jessica still squirmed with anxiety at every sympathetic customer who headed Leah's way.

Several people approached Jessica's food truck and stopped short. Then they pulled out phones and showed their screens to their friends. She knew exactly what they were sharing—news articles linking her truck to Cameron's killing.

She tried not to focus on those people. Plenty of others came her way. Perhaps the circumstances weren't as bad as she'd worried. Pippa and Madeline brought the rest of the Pankhurst family, who made conspicuous yummy noises in the direction of the film crew before giving her five stars each. Even Hattie managed to smile and say good things without causing a disaster.

After the Pankhursts' visit, Jessica forced herself to be more positive. She had the home court advantage. For every person who veered away in fright, there were two who'd known her since childhood and were excited to rate her bakes. Perhaps she could do this. She could get enough points to win.

Then she looked up at the next customer, and Jessica's hope dropped like a stone. The person standing before her was Beatrix, wearing her distinctive studded black jacket. Jessica was so startled she fumbled the cake she was holding. It slipped from her grip, landed on her shoe, and slid to the floor, leaving a thick smear of lemon curd and cream. Jessica hadn't expected anyone from her family to even acknowledge her that day, let alone come to her truck. But Beatrix wasn't here to taste her food. Without even looking at Jessica, she reached to the scoring pad and jabbed hard at the one-star button.

Jessica blinked away tears. She wouldn't let Beatrix get to her.

Then she looked up at the rest of the queue. Every person there was a member of her family, all with grim expressions that said a stream of single stars was coming Jessica's way.

The camera crew was directly behind the queue, panning up to Jessica's face. She couldn't react. She couldn't even let out the sob that rose in her chest like warm dough. She could only watch as cousins, aunts, and uncles inched closer, all ready to give her one star and ruin her chances in the contest.

Until now, she'd been holding onto a secret hope that Aunt Enriqueta's plotting about the Askew board was in vain. She'd told herself that these people wouldn't really side with her power-hungry aunt over her warm and loving grandma.

But she was getting a preview of what was to come, and the situation became scarily real.

Jessica stepped away from the hatch and grabbed her phone. Then she typed out a quick message to the renegade cousins in Hay. In it, she explained exactly what was going on and asked what they were doing that evening. Pippa's suggestion of a loud objection from any Askew she could muster had seemed extreme the night before. But now Jessica grabbed the idea with both hands.

She couldn't let Aunt Enriqueta win. She couldn't give up without a fight.

28

As the day wore on, the sun rose higher in the sky then hovered directly overhead, watching the contest with its wide, golden gaze. By early afternoon, the kitchen in Jessica's food truck was like a furnace. The metal surfaces of her countertops were hot to the touch, and her whipped-cream cake toppings softened, melted, and dribbled into puddles.

Yorkshire barm brack was a heavy, wintery food, and Jessica's flavours had tried to brighten it into a summer treat. But summer had pushed back.

She'd faced worse conditions than this, though, at waterlogged food festivals, during truck-rocking storms, and on days so cold she couldn't feel her fingers. She'd just have to get creative and decorate her next batch to order. She'd done that before, and though the wait times lengthened, people enjoyed the personal touch.

At least, they usually did. That day, when Jessica added swirls of lemon curd and whipped cream, her piping nozzle got blocked and exploded. Then, when she dotted on rosemary jelly, it dribbled messily, and she discovered that the minifridge under her sink had blown a fuse in the heat.

For the last hour of the contest, the camera must have captured a record number of shots of her panic-face. A few feet away, Leah was struggling, too, but she still had the energy to explain to customers how devastated she was by the loss of Cameron.

More five-star tokens of support entered her machine.

Jessica couldn't even find her favourite pan when she went to make an extra batch of lemon curd. If she were Cameron, she'd be shouting about sabotage. But she was too hot and already had far too many worries to add that one to her list.

Only the flashing message notifications on her phone distracted her from the panic of food preparation. She was excited to see the names of her Hay-based relatives popping up. But each one brought worse news than the last. They all replied quickly enough to show they cared. But nobody was free that evening. A cousin she'd bonded with over a long night of whiskey and chocolate cake offered to skip her best friend's hen party if she was really needed. But Jessica couldn't ask that.

She wanted to. But she couldn't.

A single, distant relative wouldn't be the powerful objection she needed to hold back her aunt's dastardly scheme anyway.

Her spirit was as broken as a dropped egg, but she forced back tears and focused on her work. Given the way the day had gone, she could very well be eliminated after this head-to-head. Leah's public star ratings had to be far higher than hers. And as Jessica tried to prepare her final cake to send to the judges, the battle between the heat in the kitchen and her bag of whipped cream was leaving her on the losing end.

But when time was called at the end of the day, she'd got a pretty good cake in the well-protected cool box to be taken along to the producers. She stepped down from her truck, brushed away the ginger curls stuck to her sweaty face, and carried the box towards the camera for the last shot of the day.

Leah walked beside her, her hands struggling so hard with her box that it looked to be filled with lead. Her steps were slow, and Jessica struggled to match her snail-like pace.

Jessica felt sorry for the young woman, who had no friends in village and who'd just lost her boyfriend tragically. No matter how bad the circumstances were in Jessica's life, at least she could run to Pippa for comforting words and some cuddles with her loving cat, Madame Poirot, that evening. Leah had nobody.

Jessica turned her head, wanting to share a smile before she and Leah took their last steps to the camera together. This episode was the final show for one of them, and whoever it was, Leah didn't have to feel alone.

But she wasn't there. Jessica slowed to a crawl, but Leah didn't catch up.

"We can do this," she said, her voice as bright as the sun that still baked overhead.

But when she looked behind, Leah wasn't just slow. She was stumbling.

She was crashing to the ground, her eyes rolling up into her head and her cake tumbling from its box and into the dirt.

The breath left Jessica's chest. Leah lay face down. She didn't move. Jessica had observed this scene before. She'd found Cameron just like this in the alley. Someone had murdered him in cold blood. Had they killed Leah too?

29

Jessica's legs weakened. She felt as fragile as meringue. She wobbled, stumbled, and struggled to catch herself, desperate not to fall onto the hard cobbles.

Her chest tightened as she fought to stay standing. She was hot—had been all day. This heat came from more than just the strong sun. She had a fever. Had she been attacked? Poisoned? Was she dying?

"An ambulance is coming," a voice called from far away. Everything was distant. Jessica was falling down a deep well. Her surroundings were dark. She fought to swim up, to stay in the world.

Hands caught her fall and lowered her to the ground.

"My cake," she mumbled as someone took her box. She'd worked so hard, and she couldn't lose everything now. Not like this.

The figures around her were blurry, and their voices were jumbled. She caught words—*rest, breathe, faint*—but they curdled in the air, refusing to blend smoothly into sentences. The voices wanted something. She was sure of that. They queried, worried, insisted. But she couldn't reply.

She dropped further into the well of unconsciousness.

No. She couldn't go. She didn't want to die like this.

But as she tried to reach up, her body grew heavier. She sank deeper. Then everything disappeared.

30

A beep echoed in the darkness. Then another.

With her hands, Jessica searched for the walls of the well, but what she found was softness. The ground beneath her was warm and cushioned, and her body longed to give into its temptation. She could rest here. She could sleep.

But then she remembered Leah collapsing. And Cameron dying the day before. She wasn't safe.

Jessica focused every ounce of effort on prising open her eyelids. They snapped shut again over a searing brightness. But she pushed back and slowly eased them open. She saw fluorescent tubes and a broad expanse of white.

Her brain felt disconnected from its usual power source. No generator was kicking in, and it seemed like any idea had to be produced by turning a crank.

Where was she?

Deep, careful thinking brought together beeps, bright lights, and what must have been a bed beneath her. A strong fragrance saturated the air—a sharp sting of disinfectant. She could be in only one place—a hospital.

She could rest here—the doctors would take care of her.

Again, she reminded herself that she wasn't safe. She couldn't lie here unprotected. Perhaps she'd survived whatever had happened to her that day, but someone was determined to take down contestants from the baking contest, and Jessica couldn't let them.

She breathed deeply and braced herself for rib pain, nausea, or the black pit of unconsciousness again. But nothing happened. The air flowed in easily, and she felt more awake. She breathed again then gingerly tensed her muscles. She moved slowly, ready for the darkness to pull her back down. But it never came.

The background throb of a headache was the only pain she could find, and that seemed to be fading. The IV bag connected to her left arm was the sole sign of treatment. She turned to look at it. But before she could focus her eyes enough to read what the bag contained, a sudden crushing sensation hit her upper body.

Her slow brain took a moment to understand someone was hugging her.

"You're awake!" The words were muffled against her back, but Jessica knew this voice as well as her own. It was Pippa, whose purple-tipped nails danced before her as the hug loosened and Jessica regained the ability to breathe.

"How long—"

Jessica didn't even finish speaking before Pippa sat on her bed and blurted everything.

"I never should have left your side today. You always work too hard. And in this heat, that can be lethal. Those aren't my words. The nurse said that. You're on a drip for dehydration, but the doctor said there wouldn't be any long-term damage. You weren't too dehydrated, she said, but the shock of seeing Leah collapse on top of that made you pass out. I told her you'd been under a lot of stress lately, and she said that can't have helped. So that's medical advice saying you have to relax. I won't let you ignore it. You've only been out for about half an hour, though it's felt like a week."

Jessica's head swam with this information. She didn't think she'd remember it all, but she caught the most significant parts—she hadn't been attacked; she was just overworked and dehydrated. That was all. Had Leah suffered from that too?

Then Jessica spotted the young baker, who was lying in the next bed. Her skin was so pale she melted into the bedding, like sugar stirred into cream. She didn't look anything like her usual rosy-cheeked self. Only her chestnut hair and its vibrant pink ends made Jessica certain the woman was her.

"She's got an infection," Pippa said, her voice low as though she thought Leah could hear it otherwise. But it didn't look like she was even close to consciousness. "A new tattoo on her shoulder got infected. Apparently, it spread to her bloodstream and could have killed her."

"Did you see it?" Jessica's brain was too slow for her to understand why she'd asked that question. But she knew the answer was important.

"The tattoo? Yes." Pippa glanced over at Leah, who still hadn't moved. "The news spread quickly that you'd been taken away in an ambulance, and I set off as soon as I heard. I cut through the back way and got here just a few minutes behind you. The doctors were evaluating Leah's infection in the ER when I came in. It looked awful. Very red and inflamed. She was shaky and feverish too. They gave her something to make her sleep, I think."

"But did you see it?" Jessica pressed. No, that wasn't the question she meant. She tried again. "What was it a tattoo of?"

"Hmmmm." Pippa cocked her head. "It was hard to tell through the redness. It was pretty small too."

But Jessica already knew. She'd seen that tattoo the day before. In fact, she'd seen it twice—once on Leah's shoulder and once on Cameron's. Her headache grew sharper as she tried to understand why this tattoo was important.

"A whisk!" Pippa said, with so much excitement it caused Leah to stir in the next bed.

Pippa's response stirred something in Jessica's mind too. She understood what was strange about Leah's situation.

"If that whisk tattoo is infected," Jessica said, as much to herself as Pippa, "it has to be brand-new. But Cameron had the exact same one."

"They were a couple, weren't they?"

Jessica nodded. She and Pippa had talked about that on the walk back from the pub the night before. During that conversation, Jessica told the Pankhurst sisters everything she'd learned about Cameron. "But I saw that tattoo on Cameron on the show's first day. He got it before he even knew Leah."

Pippa frowned, and Jessica wasn't sure whether that was a reaction to the information or to her. The detail about the mismatched tattoo timing felt like it changed everything. But she didn't know how. Her nose tingled, just as it did when she found the missing ingredient in a recipe.

Leah could have had plenty of reasons to get the same tattoo as Cameron long after him. But Jessica couldn't rid herself of the creeping feeling that something wasn't right.

This detail was as tiny as the line-draw whisk, but it held the key to Cameron's death. She was sure of it.

31

Leah stirred in her hospital bed.

"We should get out of here." Jessica felt as lost as a crumb in a carpet. Her thoughts were too muddled for her to make sense of what she'd just learned. But it wasn't good.

"The doctor said you need to rest." Pippa folded her arms with a firmness that meant business.

"My drip is nearly empty, and I feel fine."

"You're a terrible liar." Pippa stood on her tiptoes and puffed up her chest. "And if the doctor says to rest, I'm going to see that you do it."

"I just want to go back to my grandma's. I'll rest there."

"I know you must feel worried about the board meeting, but going back to Askew Avenue isn't what you need right now. You shouldn't risk your health with more stress."

The board! Jessica hadn't even thought about it. Her relatives were planning to remove her grandma from her family board that evening, and Jessica hadn't found a single way to stop them. Thoughts of this problem opened the floodgates to her worries, and they all came rushing back.

Her mind filled with images of the news linking her food truck to murder, nightmares of her grandma's reaction to that, and panic that Leah's lies about her tattoo may be hiding an even bigger secret.

Could the sweet-seeming baker be a cold-blooded killer?

"I'll rest at my grandma's, I promise. You can stay with me to make sure if you like, but—"

"Jessica?"

She whipped around and saw Leah's gaze fixed on her. Her voice was barely a whisper, and her eyes were only open a crack, but that was enough to make Jessica panic.

"Nurse!" Jessica cried out, waving at the woman in uniform at the other end of the ward. "My IV bag is empty, and I really need to go."

Pippa looked at her like she'd lost her mind. "You're meant to be staying calm, remember?"

"That's why I want to go. Hospitals are too stressful, and I just want to get out of here."

"Jessica," Leah said again, more loudly this time, and she struggled up to a sitting position. She didn't exactly look like a threat, but Jessica wanted to get space between them until she was sure Leah wasn't.

The nurse heading their way darted to Leah's side and propped up her pillows. Leah gasped sharply as she rested back on them, and her tattooed shoulder curled in protectively.

"Nurse, could you help?" Jessica looked down at the needle taped into her arm. Could she take it out herself? Her patience was as thin as parchment paper. "We really have to go. We—"

"He didn't love me," Leah said, covering her face with her hands and sobbing. "He didn't even like me. I've been such an idiot."

Jessica froze with her hand on her IV tube.

Pippa, who was addicted to every romance show from *Love is Blind* and *Married at First Sight* to *Love Island* and *Ex on the Beach*, raced to Leah's side. She perched her generous behind on the young woman's bed and leaned forwards. "Who could *not* like you? You're accomplished, beautiful, and very sweet."

"Who are—?"

"I'm Jessica's best friend. You can trust me."

Jessica was still silent—her throbbing head could make no sense of what Leah was saying.

"I really thought he had feelings for me." Leah wiped tears from her cheeks. "He flirted with me every time we met for the contest, and he sent me really thoughtful messages. But last week, he said I was too young to get serious about. That's why I got the tattoo. To show him I'm serious. And you can see where that's got me."

Pippa leaned forwards, as she always did during the juicy parts of her favourite shows. "I'd be flattered if someone did that for me. Did Cameron appreciate it?"

After another sob, Leah shook her head. "I thought he would. He'd come all the way to Little Quillington, and we planned for him to make a surprise appearance during the head-to-head contest. But when I showed him the tattoo yesterday morning, he just laughed at me. He said I was a silly little girl. I was too embarrassed to tell anybody, even after he died."

Pippa gasped. "He was just using you to worm his way back into the competition?"

Leah shook her head again in confusion. "He didn't have to. He'd already got his place back, and he was going to be on the show again next week." Then she released another sob and let Pippa wrap her in a careful hug. "I really thought he liked me."

Jessica pictured young, pretty Leah sliding down the shoulder of her cardigan and showing Cameron the whisk tattoo. His laughter must have stung. Could it have hurt enough to kill over? To someone so impulsive they'd get a tattoo for a boy they weren't even really dating, maybe.

But Billy, the police officer, had said something heavy killed Cameron. What sharp-cornered object could tiny Leah have swung with sufficient force to kill?

That question wasn't the only one Jessica had. As Leah sniffled into a tissue, Jessica asked, "If he already had his spot back in the show, why did he bother coming all this way just to pop into a background shot?"

Leah shrugged then winced, apparently at the pain in her shoulder. "I've been trying to work that out. He said that last week's sabotage was connected with someone on the crew, and he was coming here to find out who."

"But the regular crew isn't here," Jessica said, more confused than ever and wishing she'd taken Pippa's advice to rest. "Pablo's team works for the same production company, but their work is separate. He must have known that. So what was he here for?"

"That's what I've been trying to understand." Leah took a long, slow breath. "I think he was lying about his reason for coming. I'm pretty sure he came here because of you."

32

Jessica's skull throbbed at full strength—it felt like a ten-pound bag of flour was pressing down on it. What did Leah mean? How could Cameron have come here because of Jessica? She didn't really know him. After he was out of the show, she'd never expected to see him again.

"Did he..." Jessica struggled to form a thought through the pain roaring in her head. She pressed her fingers to her temples. "Did he think I sabotaged him? No, it can't be that. I'm not a crew member, and...and..."

A grey-haired woman in a smart skirt and blouse strode over to Jessica before Leah could respond. "I understand you're wanting to be discharged."

"This is the doctor," Pippa whispered. That was obvious, but given the state of Jessica's brain, she was glad her friend was making sure she understood.

Jessica forced a smile. "Yes, I'm fully rehydrated, and I'd like to go home and..." She didn't know what she'd do after she left. The last couple of days had been a whirlwind of confusion. A few moments earlier, she'd thought Leah was dangerous, but now it seemed like the young woman had important information.

"You don't look quite back to full strength." While feeling Jessica's wrist to take her pulse, the doctor leaned down and peered into her eyes. "I'd be happier if you could stick around for a few hours. Is your head bothering you?"

Jessica didn't have a few hours. As Pippa had just reminded her, the Askew board meeting would be held after the shops shut at eight, and the clock on the wall said it was long past four already. She had no idea what she could achieve before the meeting, but she couldn't sit here in the hospital and wait for her grandma's fate to be decided. "No, it's just quite warm in here."

The doctor looked at the full ward, which was indeed rather hot and stuffy. "Well, if someone can stay with you till tomorrow, I suppose you should be fine to go."

Pippa stood up quickly. "I'll look after her."

The doctor nodded then strode away and called over her shoulder, "Wait for the nurse's final check. Then you're good to leave."

Jessica swivelled her legs off the bed.

"She said wait." Pippa put out a hand and squared her feet as though she could really block Jessica's path.

"I will. I just need to speak to Leah." She looked at the exhausted woman in the bed beside her. "What do you mean Cameron came here because of me?"

"I'm so sorry," Leah said, cradling her sore shoulder and wincing at the pain. "I should have told you earlier. No, I should have stopped him. I just didn't know what he was going to do."

"What did he do?"

"He went into that shop we were sitting outside yesterday." Leah's words were laboured, but she forced herself on. "The one that angry woman came out of."

"That's my aunt. She owns Criminally Good Mysteries."

"I promise I didn't... didn't know what he was planning when he went in there. Cameron just said he wanted to... to talk to the person who owned it. I didn't know she was related to you."

"Did Cameron know that?" Learning the fact wouldn't have been hard. Her family made their living from visitors to their bookish community. There was plenty of information online, and much had been made of Jessica's ties when she first appeared on the baking contest.

"He... seemed to, yes. He told her he..." Leah shuffled to sit straighter, wincing as she jostled her elbow. "He said he wanted information about you."

Jessica was glad she was sitting down. She felt like Lewis Carroll's Alice, stepping through a mirror into a world that was impossible to understand. "From my aunt?"

Leah blinked slowly, looking ready to fall asleep. "He asked if she knew something that could get you kicked off the show."

Pippa gasped like this scenario was the worst wedding-day betrayal on *Love is Blind*. "But he already had his spot back. He didn't need to get someone kicked off for a place."

"He was sure Jessica would win. She's a better baker than him."

"So he was going to dig up dirt on her?"

Leah nodded. A little colour returned to her cheeks, but it wasn't the glow of good health. It looked more like embarrassment for the part she'd played by being with him.

Jessica thought back to the day before. "Aunt Enriqueta shouted at you yesterday. She called Cameron a no-good young man, but she's not exactly my biggest fan. If he was trying to dig up dirt on me, she'd be the first person to share it." Her heart fluttered at the possibility that her aunt had defended her. Perhaps she'd stood up to Cameron's attempts.

"I... I think she would have told him some things." Leah's pink cheeks deepened to a fiery red. This subject was clearly hard for her to talk about. Was that because of what Aunt Enriqueta revealed? Leah gripped her bedsheets as she struggled against what must have been her tired body's call to sleep. "But he pulled out a letter someone had sent him. He said if she didn't give him the information he wanted, he'd share its contents with the press."

"A letter?" Pippa echoed.

"What was in it?" Jessica asked simultaneously.

Leah shook her head. Limp waves of hair brushed against her slack face. No longer able to keep her eyes open, she murmured, "I wasn't close enough to see it. But Cameron read some out loud... Then she... That's when... Kicked us out." Leah's head dropped to her chest.

Jessica was as lost as a sprinkle of sugar in a snowstorm. These past couple of days had already brought incredible shocks. But this situation was utterly incomprehensible.

The only thing Jessica understood was that this matter couldn't be good.

33

"A letter," Jessica said for the hundredth time as Pippa drove her home. "Why would Cameron have a letter that shocked Aunt Enriqueta? What could it possibly say?"

She'd asked Leah as much, but the young woman couldn't stay awake to answer. Leah had mumbled through her medicated haze about cream notepaper and something involving a typewriter, then she'd repeated the word "angry" as she slipped into sleep.

"Who even sends letters these days?" Pippa asked, drumming her fingers on the wheel while waiting for the light to change. "And they used a typewriter? I'd have kept my dad's business going if I'd known typewriters were making a comeback."

"We need to get hold of that letter. It links Cameron to Little Quillington, so it must be tied to his death." Was that true? The idea that Cameron was connected to her aunt felt so impossibly strange—the clues in this case were as crumbly as stale cake—but it had to mean something. "If we had it, could you tell what make of machine it was written on? That might tell us who wrote it."

"Isn't that just in the movies? And how would you even get the letter? Cameron probably had it in his pocket when he died, so the police will—"

"Perfect!" When Jessica signed the filming permit that morning, Billy had given her a copy of the paperwork. It had his contact details on, and she pulled out her phone now and rang him.

"You're after a letter?" the young officer asked, as though he'd never heard of such a thing.

"Yes, I think it could have been in Cameron's pocket."

"So that's what that was. Huh. He'd got some paper in there, but it was soaked in blood, and it fell apart when we took it out." He surprised Jessica by asking a follow-up question. "Who was it from?"

"Leah," she answered before thinking. "It was... a love letter, and I said I'd ask for it back. But I'll let her know it's not possible."

Jessica hung up as Pippa pulled away from the lights and drove onto the moor-top road. The view outside was desolate. This place was the landscape of Cathy and Heathcliff from *Wuthering Heights*—moody, hill-stamping characters written by Emily Brontë in nearby Haworth. Jessica knew just how they felt.

"I'm sorry," Pippa said, her sympathetic face making clear she'd heard every word. "How about we load up on snacks and have a Julia Child binge? I'll even let you rewatch the bit where she drops the potato pancake, and you tell me that everyone always thinks she dropped a turkey."

Jessica felt as tempted as she would be by a slice of her favourite carrot cake. But she pushed herself to sit up straight.

"No. That won't be necessary. The police confirmed that Cameron *did* have the letter in his pocket, and that's all I need."

"For what?"

Jessica cracked a window and took a deep breath from outside. She let the cool moor-top air fill her lungs. "To fight Aunt Enriqueta."

Pippa slowed down. "I told the doctor I'd take care of you. I don't think that includes helping you break into a police station, if that's what you're planning."

"No. The letter's ruined, but it doesn't matter if I actually have it. It's enough for Aunt Enriqueta to think I do."

"Extremely sneaky! I'm impressed. But..." After checking her mirrors, Pippa pulled into a layby on the thin ribbon of road. "I don't really know how to ask this, but are you sure you want to confront your aunt?"

"I have to. There's something in that letter that scared her. If she thinks I've got it, I can stop her pushing my grandma off the board."

"Or maybe..." Pippa trailed off again, which wasn't like her. She could be counted on to share her deepest secrets in a heartbeat.

"Maybe what? If she's angry at me, what's the worst she could do? She's already pushing out the only relative who supports me."

"She was angry at Cameron." Pippa's words came slowly, and she fiddled with her car's vents, adjusted the angle of her rearview mirror, and retied her tree-shaped air freshener. "And look what happened to him."

34

Aunt Enriqueta had been angry at Cameron, and a few hours later, he'd wound up dead. Jessica tried to connect those two points. There was a clear line of causation between them, of course, but her mind wouldn't draw it. Aunt Enriquetta was angry, sour, cruel, and all manner of other horrible things. But surely, she wasn't a killer.

Was she?

Just the idea pulled Jessica's brain taut enough to snap. She focused on it in silence while Pippa drove them back to Little Quillington.

Aunt Enriqueta ate quail-egg and watercress sandwiches. She carefully folded and reused wrapping paper. She wore a necklace hidden under her dress, which Jessica knew held a pair of wedding rings. Aunt Enriqueta was a person, with the habits and contradictions of a rounded life. Murderers weren't like that. They were villains who had to be hunted down and locked up. But, now that Jessica thought of it, that idea came from the mysteries she'd read as a kid, which featured greedy moustache-twirlers who'd stop at nothing. Maybe, in real life, anyone could kill if pushed hard enough.

Jessica had no clue what was in the letter Cameron had shown Aunt Enriqueta, or even who'd sent it. According to Leah, Aunt Enriqueta had been angry about it. Jessica herself had experienced the woman shouting about Cameron in the street. Then she'd been sneaking up from the tunnels as though she was hiding something. Could she really be a killer?

"We can check the footage from yesterday," Jessica said, her brain once more surprising her with a useful notion. "I was with Aunt Enriqueta for most of the time after I left your shop. She was on camera with me in the middle of the square. Then it was time for the parade, and she disappeared. I saw her from the back as she walked away, and I thought she was heading to Askew Avenue, but if she didn't, that's when she must have..."

"Killed him."

"Right. The camerawoman and the mic operator got separated by the crowd. I didn't see where they ended up, but if the camera kept rolling, it might have caught something."

"That's not the world's best lead," Pippa said.

"It's better than nothing. We need to see yesterday's recording. It's our only chance to discover if Aunt Enriqueta could have done this."

Pippa pulled onto Inkwell Lane, the winding road that connected the moor-top route with Little Quillington. As she drove past her sister's church, the clock struck five.

"It's the summer fête weekend!" Jessica looked up at the large church clock and checked that the five loud chimes were correct.

"You already had this realisation. Yesterday. Do I need to take you back to the hospital to get your head examined?"

"No, I mean you need to get back to Just My Type. You're open late today." As they drove into the centre of village, the door of every business they passed was wide open. On the fête weekend, the shops took advantage of the influx of visitors by staying open till at least eight. Some proprietors even served snacks and drinks and welcomed customers until ten.

"It's taken care of."

Madeline was the only person Pippa usually let watch her shop when she wasn't around. But on Sunday, the vicar was surely not free. "Did you close early? You'll get a penalty from the council."

"No, I didn't close early." Pippa kept her eyes fixed on the road.

"You don't mean…"

"She'll be fine."

"She's never fine." Jessica knew exactly who was in charge of the shop right then, and nothing good would come of the situation. "Hattie doesn't know the meaning of the word 'fine.'"

Pippa's pinched expression as she parked said she, too, was worried. "She's really been a lot better recently. Don't worry about it."

Jessica thought but did not say that *a lot* better wasn't nearly good enough. Hattie was like an oven with a broken thermostat—out of control to the point of being dangerous. She was named after Harriet the Spy, and when she'd been little, her snooping attempts to copy the character she was named for had been sweet. But as she'd grown up, she'd lost all understanding of privacy and respect for boundaries. Jessica wouldn't trust her to look after Madame Poirot, let alone the shop the cat lived in.

Jessica wanted to tell Pippa to return to Just My Type and rescue her neat storeroom from her sister's invasion, but she bit back her words. She didn't think she could face the next step alone.

"Sorry. I'm sure she'll be OK," Jessica said. "Everything seems so serious all of a sudden. That's all. This time last week, I was fretting over a baked Alaska that hadn't turned out perfectly. Now, I need to somehow get hold of a tape that might point to my aunt having murdered someone she had no reason to even know. And even if it turns out she's not a killer, she's still trying to kick her own mother off the Askew board, and every relative in village is on her side. Things feel far, far too real."

Pippa wrapped her up in a tight hug, which soothed some of Jessica's fears. But she hadn't even shared what step of her plan gave her the sharpest prickle of dread. She was scared to confront Pablo. In many ways, he was the usual, self-interested TV type. But she couldn't forget how quickly he'd tried to turn suspicion on her when she'd discovered Cameron's body.

If she hadn't known exactly where he was in the moments before Cameron's death—pinned to a lamppost in fear of the children milling about—she might have considered him a suspect. But even if he wasn't one, there was something she didn't trust about Pablo. She was glad to have Pippa by her side as she walked into the village square to look for him.

If he was still in Little Quillington, the village square was surely where he'd be, looking for a story he could spin into a documentary. Within moments, she spotted the flash of a camera lens and knew she'd guessed correctly. But then a muffled sob caught her attention, and she and Pippa raced towards it.

35

When Jessica spotted Pablo, Mrs Merdle was waving her rolling pin at him, and his face showed a mix of confusion and defiance. Jessica had seen this exact moment before. Hadn't she? Perhaps she did have to go back to the hospital for a head check.

But as she got closer, she realised the situation was nothing like last time.

"You give that poor girl a break," Mrs Merdle scolded, putting her bulky arm around the camerawoman's bent waist and guiding her to a bench. "She's seen nothing but bodies, bodies, bodies. People have been dropping like flies everywhere you've dragged her." At those words, several early-evening shoppers in the square gave Mrs Merdle an alarmed look. But she glared at them so sharply they kept walking. Jessica watched the brightly dressed tourists shrug and shake their heads. In Little Quillington, so many literary events were happening all the time that this interaction could be a play rehearsal or some other bookish activity.

"There's actually only been one body," Pablo said. "The other two people you've heard about merely fainted. And in fact, here's one of them now, and look, she's totally fine."

Jessica was flustered by Pablo's magician's-assistant flourish as she approached. She wasn't "totally fine." Leah wasn't fine *at all*, and she certainly hadn't "merely fainted," but Jessica didn't want to get into that. She had something far more important to worry about.

Mrs Merdle lifted the camera down from the shoulder of the woman on the bench. She looked tiny without it, but she had to be strong. Even Mrs Merdle, who got plenty of practice wielding her rolling pin with force, struggled to lower the camera gently to the ground.

"She's had a shock, and you're not giving the young lass a minute of peace." Mrs Merdle's fit of kindness edged towards its true purpose. She was a dedicated believer that her enemy's enemy was her friend, and she was fond of making alliances against those she disliked. As she patted the camerawoman's powerful shoulder, she rounded on Pablo with renewed force. "People like you can't give *any*body peace, and I won't stand for it."

The camerawoman hiccupped and scrubbed her sturdy glove across her face. The jacket she wore was thick for such a warm day. She must have needed it to protect her shoulder from the camera she carried. Had the heat that day got to her too?

"Do you need a drink?" Pippa asked, appearing with a cool can of lemonade she must have grabbed from her shop. Jessica hoped the speed with which she'd returned meant Hattie hadn't destroyed the place.

As Pippa and Mrs Merdle set about soothing the overwhelmed camerawoman, Jessica sidled up to Pablo. In as casual a voice as she could muster, she said, "I thought you'd be headed back to London by now."

His shrug was casual too. But the glint of opportunity shone in his gaze. There was a story far more interesting than any baking-show gig here, and he wanted to get something out of it. "It's been a dramatic couple of days. We're just going to get a few shots in and learn more about your lovely village before travelling back."

She knew what "learn more" meant to someone like Pablo. He was going to spin this weekend's story into something lurid he could sell on the side.

"If you're looking to capture Little Quillington, you're on the right track with Mrs Merdle. She knows everything and everyone around here."

"She's... uhhh... not my biggest fan." He gestured to the bench, where the apron-clad woman was telling the camerawoman how hard she seemed to have it while glaring daggers at Pablo.

"She's a softie, really, if you know how to handle her." That response was only a medium-sized exaggeration, not a flat-out lie.

Pablo looked at Jessica from the corner of his eye. "And you know how to do that?"

"I might." She waited until Pablo turned to face her completely. "And I'm happy to help in exchange for a favour."

"I'm listening."

He listened well, and within a couple of minutes, he'd got a laptop out of his bag. Jessica felt as sapped as a squeezed lemon, but she directed all her attention on his screen.

She saw the square full of toddling bees from the morning before. The sun-drenched scene panned to a close-up of her and Aunt Enriqueta. She sped through this and watched with hawklike focus. Their interview ended, and her aunt walked out of the shot. But then the camera was jostled and spun, and as it turned around, it caught the distinctive stiff shoulders of her aunt's black-clad back. Jessica watched the woman cross the square and head directly down Askew Avenue.

It was definitive. She didn't go anywhere near the place where Cameron was killed. The camera wobbled after she walked away, then it pivoted towards Verse View, where there was a flash of a white T-shirt, then the shot cut out.

"Go back," Jessica said. Her heart raced at what she'd just seen.

"I kept up my end. Now it's your turn."

"I need a pen and paper. While you're getting them, I'm watching this again."

He rummaged in his bag and pulled them out. Jessica barely looked away from the screen as she scribbled down a list then thrust it at Pablo. "What's this?"

"Give it to Mrs Merdle, and she'll do anything you ask."

"Sugar... butter... milk. Is this a shopping list?"

"Guard it with your life. That's the scone recipe I won with at the summer fête three years in a row. Mrs Merdle's been trying to get that prize for decades, and with this, she'll take next year's crown."

Pablo walked away, muttering something about country bumpkins.

Jessica ignored him and stared at the final frame frozen on the screen. Before her was the best shot through the crowd towards Verse View. Behind the clutch of people, just metres away, was a blur of white clothing. Was it Cameron's top, beneath which his heart was closing in on its final beat? Jessica stared at the image, wondering if the killer, too, was standing in plain sight.

She scanned each face. There was a mix of excited tourists and long-familiar locals. Nobody's expression had an ounce of malice in it. But someone right there was moments from murder.

36

Jessica looked at her watch. She felt like she'd been staring at the laptop screen for days, but it was only five fifteen. Her aunt's board meeting was less than three hours away, and now Jessica was confident that her aunt wouldn't kill her for trying to stop it.

She wasn't sure whether someone else might kill her, though—she'd still got no idea what had happened to Cameron. His death was tied to her aunt, somehow, and Jessica's brain was exhausted trying to find the link. Her tired eyes closed on her view of the screen.

But then Pippa raced over and woke her with a loud, "No! Tell me that wasn't the real recipe. Did you really give the secret to your magic scones to Mrs Merdle?"

"They're not magic. They're just very good. I've offered you the recipe before, but—"

Pippa held up a hand. "I'm a scone eater, not a scone maker." Then she swung her arm out wide. "Mrs Merdle already owns everything the light touches."

"Not quite, Mufasa."

"And if she wins the scone crown at next year's fête, she'll have absolute power."

"Mrs Merdle's dominion over Little Quillington is a problem for another day. Right now, I need to tackle issues a little closer to home. My first stop is Just My Type. If the place is still standing, that is."

"You should have more trust in Hattie. She's always really liked you."

"That ball of chaos has a funny way of showing it. Anyway, I just need to use one of your dad's old typewriters. If that's OK?"

Pippa's eyes sparkled as she and Jessica crossed the square and headed down Verse View. She'd always wanted to continue her father's business, but in the modern era, typewriters didn't bring in enough for a living. "All the working ones were sold off years ago. But there's one in the window I've been tinkering with. I might be able to get it usable if you don't mind the letters being a little bit crooked."

"That's perfect." Jessica braced herself as she walked towards Just My Type—doing so felt like opening the oven door to check the results of a new recipe. There was no way to know what Hattie would do from one moment to the next. The floor of the shop could have been converted into an ice rink, every bulb might have been replaced with a pink one, and the items in the storeroom would perhaps be laid out for a penny apiece. Hattie would explain everything as though it were perfectly reasonable, and she never learned from her mistakes.

"Back again!" Pippa called as she went in first. "And Jessica's with me."

Her bright, singsongy voice and advanced warning about Jessica indicated that Pippa didn't have quite as much faith in her sister as she claimed.

"Perfect timing," Hattie said, darting out from behind the counter. "Oooh, no, wait, let me bring this out here. I've just finished it, and I think you're both going to love it. Like, really flip!"

Hattie was the shortest of the Pankhurst sisters, and her crouching scurry always made her seem like a mouse stealing cheese. From a high corner, Madame Poirot, the shop cat, tracked Hattie's every move.

The feeling of worry walking in was nothing compared to the open-mouthed shock Jessica experienced when Hattie lifted a gigantic, flattened cardboard box onto the counter. She laid it down to reveal a collage made of dozens and dozens of photos, every one of them featuring Jessica.

The red-headed baker grabbed Pippa's arm.

Pippa grabbed her right back. "Hattie, what is that? It looks like something a serial killer made."

"What?" Hattie cocked her head and gazed down at her work. "That's not what it looks like. I just used those papers and magazines you'd collected. I thought this was what you were planning to do with them. Why else would you have gathered so many articles about Jess?"

Jessica and Pippa shuffled forwards and leaned in for a closer look at the collage that covered the entire counter. The project did look quite murdery, but Jessica saw now that the photos and articles were indeed from the stack of papers she'd put there the day before—the ones Pippa had saved and kept on display. They showed Jessica holding up cakes, wafting a baking tray, serving customers, and even serving leftovers to the hardworking crew. She smiled at the photograph of the camerawoman caught with a mouthful of chocolate cake—Meg could never resist.

"That's so..." Pippa squeezed her best friend's arm. "It's so thoughtful, isn't it?"

"It's something."

"Yay, me!" Hattie jumped and clapped her hands like a little kid. "I measured it before I started, because I'm trying to get better at thinking before I act. This fits perfectly on the front of the counter here, so—"

"No!" Jessica and Pippa said in unison. Then Pippa added, "It'd get ruined in such a high-traffic area. I think this is something for the storeroom. Why don't you take it there now? In fact, could you make some peanut butter sandwiches while you're out back? We haven't eaten in hours, and I've got a typewriter to fix."

Jessica's stomach rumbled, though not in eager anticipation of eating something prepared by Hattie. This rumble was a nervous one. A photo of the show's semifinalists in the collage made her think of the next part of her plan—one she wasn't certain of at all.

She needed to get more information about Cameron's letter, and there was only one person to ask: Leah. If the young woman was still sleeping, Jessica didn't know where else to turn. She picked up her phone and hovered over the button to dial.

When Hattie brought in the sandwiches, Jessica waited until Pippa had tried hers and smiled before tucking in. A memory of raspberry jam and anchovies still stuck with Jessica from the last time she'd tried Hattie's food, but Pippa chewed and swallowed eagerly.

Jessica bit in absentmindedly while focusing on her phone. Then she stopped and looked at the meal, which wasn't the simple peanut butter sandwich it seemed. She peeled back a slice of bread and spotted grated apple, raisins, and a sprinkle of cinnamon, all between two neatly cut slices of sourdough. The results were delicious.

She couldn't spend too long being impressed by Hattie's work, however. She needed to speak to Leah, and she couldn't put it off another moment. Jessica dialled.

37

She pressed her phone tightly to her ear and wished hard for Leah to answer. But all she heard was ring after ring.

Then a message buzzed in—"Sorry, I'm being taken for tests. I can't talk now."

Jessica wanted to shout in frustration, but a pair of customers walked into Just My Type right at that moment.

Hattie bounced behind the counter, eager to serve, and Jessica went to the window, where Pippa was working on the typewriter.

She was about to tell Pippa to stop—that her plan was already failing—when another message came in, this one from Leah.

As Hattie chatted with the day-trippers about the good weather and the delicious taste of local honey, Jessica and Pippa's eyes burned into the screen.

"She's awake!" Jessica whispered. But her joy at the sight was as fleeting as a sugar high.

I've been thinking hard about the letter Cameron had, she wrote. *I can't remember the exact words of it, but I know what part made your aunt angry.*

Jessica stared at the typing dots as she waited, waited, waited.

The letter said your family isn't what it seems.

Jessica and Pippa stared at each other in open-mouthed silence and stayed that way until the shop door opened and closed.

They sat a beat longer to be sure no more customers were inside, then they spoke at the same time.

"What?"

"I don't understand."

"How is my family tied up with this death? And what does it mean by 'they're not what they seem'?" Jessica was mystified by the Askews' entanglement in the mystery. If someone knew a secret about them, why didn't that person reveal it themselves? And what could the secret be? Her relatives spent their lives in books. To them, a terrible crime was leaving a paperback face down or spilling coffee on its pages. And how did any of this information relate to Cameron? "I'm so confused by everything."

Hattie raced over from the counter. "I've also got no idea what's going on, but I'm outraged about whatever it is! Would more sandwiches fix anything?"

Despite herself, Jessica smiled. "I think this is one of the rare problems that can't be solved by food. But at least I know a little of what the letter says. I can type up something passable and confront Aunt Enriqueta with it. Then, hopefully, I'll finally get some answers that will let me fix this mess."

38

Jessica had no idea where Cameron's letter had come from, and most of its contents were a mystery. But that wasn't important. She had a plan.

Jessica was named after a character in *The Merchant of Venice*. In fact, Shakespeare had created her name for that play. She knew several sections of it by heart, and those would be perfect for her purposes.

On the wobbly old typewriter, she tapped out, "Alack, what heinous sin is it in me to be ashamed to be my father's child?"

A few more similarly dramatic lines, full of *sins* and *secrets* and *shame*, with all the names replaced by *Askew*, created something she hoped would pass at a glance for the real letter Cameron had shown her aunt. The only real words from his letter were at the top of the page: *Your family is not what it seems.*

Jessica folded the letter, laid it against her leg, and pressed her elbow into the paper. After flattening it back out again, it looked suitably crumpled, and she pushed it into her pocket and headed for the door.

"Are you sure I can't come with you?" Pippa asked with the weariness of one who already knew the answer.

"If all goes well, I'll be back in a matter of minutes."

Hattie sprang over to the storeroom. "Pippa and I can put up the collage of you while you're away."

"If I don't make it back, that'll be an excellent memorial."

"Don't joke." Pippa gave Jessica a fierce hug that pressed the air from her lungs.

She felt the ghost of her friend's arms around her as she crossed the square and turned onto Askew Avenue. It was six o'clock, the time when the shops here would usually be closing. But this was the summer-fête weekend, so the closure was still a couple of hours away—as was the Askew board meeting.

Jessica had been tempted to wait until the last minute to confront her aunt. But if her idea didn't work, she wanted time for Plan B... whatever that might be.

As the church bells chimed six in the distance, Jessica knocked hard on the glass front of her aunt's bookshop. The display in it was a celebration of Ngaio Marsh, whose lurid book covers were as bright as a sweetshop's selection. Jessica felt like a little kid clutching her pocket money as she waited for the door to open.

Aunt Enriqueta strode across her shop. When she saw who was knocking on her window, she stopped short. Rather than shout at her to go away, Aunt Enriqueta simply stood in the entrance, slowly pushed the door open, and looked at Jessica.

"I... I know about your board meeting."

Aunt Enriqueta's dark eyes flickered. She'd concealed her plotting—travelling by tunnel and making her dastardly move when Jessica's grandma was out of town—but she barely reacted to Jessica's discovery of her plans. Did that mean it was too late? "What has inspired the sudden interest in the family's business?"

Jessica's throat tightened as she felt the sharp blade of her aunt's full attention. "I... I'm here to stop you stealing my grandma's board seat."

Aunt Enriqueta's thin lips twitched into a smile. "You are somebody without a presence or an ally on the board, so I fail to see how you might achieve that. What happens behind closed doors is out of the control of the likes of you."

Jessica pushed away the pang of longing for her grandma, who could never speak to anyone this way. Her shoulders tightened as Aunt Enriqueta's sharp eyes pierced through her. "The board won't be meeting today. You're going to cancel the session."

"What might possess me to do that?"

Jessica reached into her pocket and pulled out the cream notepaper with her typed letter on it. She unfolded it and held it up, keeping her adrenaline-flushed fingers as still as possible so her aunt could see the crooked letters and the Askew name, even from several feet away. "I don't think you want anyone seeing the letter Cameron showed you yesterday."

Aunt Enriqueta's lips trembled then pinched into an expression of genuine worry. "Where did you get that?"

Jessica flicked her gaze in the direction of Verse View. Pippa had been correct earlier when she'd said Jessica was a terrible liar. If she tried to lie now, her aunt would see through it. Instead, she hoped her eyes suggested she'd taken the letter from Cameron when she found him in Index Alley. Just My Type was close enough that her gesture wasn't technically a lie.

Aunt Enriqueta left her shop, letting the door drop shut on the way. With a flap of black fabric, she closed the distance between her and Jessica.

"Give that to me."

"Call off the meeting."

"If I do, will you give me the letter?"

Jessica's fingers pinched the paper tightly. She couldn't give it to her aunt. With anything more than a cursory glance, she'd realise it was fake.

"I'll do better than that." Jessica folded the letter and pulled a lighter from her pocket. "I'll burn it right here, so nobody else will ever see what it says. But first, I want to know where it came from." That piece of information had to bring her to the killer in this case. "Who sent this to Cameron?"

With a stiff and unreadable expression, Aunt Enriqueta looked up and down the cobbled street and waited for a gaggle of book shoppers to pass by. "I have not yet ascertained that fact."

"Don't lie to me."

The black-clad woman flicked her knife-sharp eyes to Jessica's. Those eyes held a fear that Jessica had never seen before. "I would not conceal the truth in a matter as serious as this," Aunt Enriqueta said.

Jessica held up the folded letter. She wished she could do more with it. This piece of paper felt like the key to Cameron's murder. But this version was fake, she reminded herself. She'd typed it, and if her aunt knew nothing more about it, then it was useless. Jessica held the lighter underneath it.

"Call Beatrix now and tell her to cancel the board meeting. Then I'll make this problem disappear."

In moments, Jessica heard the ringing of phones up and down the street as Beatrix passed the news around. Then she flicked her lighter—one she used for birthday candles and relaxing incense, but which now felt heavy with significance—and she watched her forgery turn to ash and smoke.

AND THEN THERE WERE SCONES 153

Her issues with Aunt Enriqueta wouldn't end here, she knew. But for now, the woman's threat against her grandma had passed. Jessica's tight chest felt no relief at this knowledge.

She'd ticked one problem off her list, but she still had a murder to solve, and she didn't have a single clue how to go about it.

39

Jessica recrossed the square with a squint of suspicion at every person she passed. Pablo and his crew had disappeared, presumably with Mrs Merdle. They'd be off filming some documentary about the dark secrets of Little Quillington. Until this weekend, Jessica didn't believe the place had any. But now, there seemed to be more than she could handle.

Although the sun had dropped low, the temperature was still as hot as an oven. Sweat trickled down Jessica's back, and the throb in the base of her skull told her she needed to drink something or end up in hospital again. She raced towards Just My Type and could almost taste the cool sweetness of the drinks in its fridge. Jessica rushed through the door and—

She stumbled backwards. Her heart raced in shock at the scene before her. She couldn't believe it. She couldn't even fully understand it.

Hattie swung her arms and aimed a huge box right at Pippa's head.

"No!" Jessica bent and charged towards the tiny, unpredictable woman, who seemed to have finally snapped. "Get away from her!"

"Wait!

"Stop!"

Jessica blocked out Hattie's cries as she barrelled into her, hooked her arms around her waist, and tackled the violent woman to the floor.

"No!" Pippa called. "Jessica, stop! Can't you hear me? I'm saying stop."

Jessica couldn't hear those words, in fact. She'd landed in a heap, and Hattie's arm was covering her head. Her heartbeat was so loud in her ears it blocked out almost every sound. But she could feel Pippa's hands pulling her away from Hattie, who sat up and giggled.

"I must have looked pretty convincing," Hattie said, rubbing her elbow then scrambling to her feet. "Maybe one of your TV contacts can get me an acting gig."

"What?" Jessica asked, untangling her long legs and standing up shakily. "What's going on?"

"We were acting out the murder," Pippa said, picking up the box Hattie had swung at her. She tossed it into the air. The box flew high, and she caught it with ease. Jessica realised it was made of cardboard.

"I had one of my brain waves," Hattie said. "And I thought we could figure out what killed the baking guy—"

"Cameron," Jessica added.

"Right. If we knew *what* killed him, we could figure out who did it."

"But the police said it could take weeks for the lab results to determine the weapon. All we know is young Officer Billy thinks it's something metal with a sharp corner." She'd told Pippa about that on the way back from the hospital, and neither of them had come up with any idea what the murder weapon might be.

"It had to have been big," Hattie said. "Heavy, too, if it cut open an enormous gash and bashed the guy's brains enough to kill him."

Jessica's stomach churned, and she pressed a hand to it to keep her recently eaten sandwich from lurching upwards. "But that can't be what happened. Somebody would have seen that so close to the square." A quiver travelled from her stomach up her spine. "How could nobody have noticed?"

Hattie hopped over to Pippa and grabbed the box. "My question exactly. Because to hit a fully grown man with something big and heavy, you have to get a real swing." She demonstrated on her sister once again, miming the action of slamming the cardboard directly into the side of her head.

Pippa nodded. "We tested it."

"We were very thorough." Hattie nodded towards the pile of sharp-cornered items piled up on the counter. Everything from juice cartons to sardine tins had been tried, but each one was clearly too small.

"And," Pippa said softly, "I'm the one who had to scrub the last traces of blood off the steps this morning. The blood didn't actually start on the steps outside my door. There was a thin trail of it leading there, which suggested Cameron was attacked right at the edge of the square."

"But how did nobody see?" A shiver ran over Jessica's scalp, and she held her breath as the sensation sank deeper and tingled through her nose. She had the same feeling she'd experienced the evening before, when Madeline suggested adding ginger to her cake recipe. The question she'd just asked felt tantalisingly close to a realisation. But how could that be? The question all along had been how Cameron was killed just metres from a bustling crowd. Nothing about this was new.

The air in the shop was perfectly still, though. It thickened like roux around the three women, and they caught one another's eyes as though words might scare the solution away.

"How did nobody see?" Jessica murmured. Then she thought again about the murder weapon—it was something large, with sharp, metal edges, that nobody would blink an eye at if it was swung in public.

The tingle in her nose turned into a whole-body shudder as she realised what had happened. She knew how Cameron had been killed.

40

Jessica knew what had killed Cameron, which meant she also knew *who* had done it. But she could not turn the spark of knowledge that fizzed around her brain into words, because the idea made no sense.

She'd spent the past couple of days chasing after people Cameron knew from the baking contest and the strange connection between him and her family, and the fact she'd just realised didn't tie into any of that.

Yet she was sure she was correct about the killer's identity.

Jessica pulled out her phone and once again dialled the number of young Officer Billy. She told him to come to Little Quillington, but when he asked why, she couldn't explain.

Instead, she walked outside, back into the sweltering evening.

Pippa followed, leaving Hattie to watch the shop. "I know that face. Usually, it means you've cracked a tricky recipe, but right now, I'm thinking it's something far less delicious."

Jessica nodded, though she wasn't fully listening. She was focusing her senses on something else—attuned to the ingredients of the world around her, teasing them apart in search of the missing, tantalising—aha!

"There, now, isn't that better?" The voice belonged to Mrs Merdle, and Jessica followed it along a path she'd walked just the day before.

This time, she ran towards Index Alley, where she found the short, stout woman adjusting a cushion beneath the camerawoman's heavy equipment.

"I told you this heat is no good for you," Mrs Merdle continued. "That thick jacket can't be doing any good, even if it does keep the camera from harming your shoulder. Mr Fancy Director here should have been looking after his crew enough to tell you that. This bit of padding is far better for the job."

At the end of the alley, four figures faced away from Jessica—Mrs Merdle, Pablo, the camerawoman, and the mic operator. Every one of them was familiar to her. But there was one significant, new thing she could see from this position.

On the camerawoman's shoulder, now that it was no longer covered by a thick, protective jacket, was a small, line-drawn tattoo. Jessica's eyes burned into the image, which she had expected but was still shocked to see. It was a whisk.

Jessica was sure that under her sturdy gloves, the woman had another familiar piece of ink—the slightly faded band of a wedding ring.

The camerawoman's whisk tattoo did not come as a surprise, but Jessica's steps still faltered when she saw it. They almost froze when she allowed her gaze to travel a few inches up to the object balanced on the woman's shoulder.

The item was large and heavy with sharp metal corners. It was her camera, and it had been hiding in plain sight all along.

Jessica couldn't count how many times she'd seen it swing around sharply, and she'd never once thought about how dangerous it could be.

The camera was a watcher. Despite its large size, it moved without being seen.

Jessica had even viewed the recording it made as it approached Cameron mere moments before his death, and she hadn't made the connection. She'd had no cause to. The camerawoman was barely a real person to her—she was an extension of the machine she carried. Jessica had spent hours in her company over the past couple of days and didn't know so much as the camerawoman's name.

She'd been closer to the crew she'd filmed with regularly for weeks, and as Jessica thought back to them now, she realised something. One of the camerawomen there, Meg, a sweet young woman who loved anything chocolatey, looked very similar to the person before her.

Jessica's nose tingled once again. The two camerawomen were from different crews, but Jessica's mind was trying to tie them together. How were they linked? And did that have anything to do with Cameron's death? She needed to learn more if she was going to solve this mystery.

"Have you guys heard from Leah?" Jessica asked, without a clue where her question would go.

The group in the alley jumped like drops of water in a hot skillet. Being at the scene of a murder clearly set everyone on edge, not just the killer.

Pablo ran a hand through his hair. "Production's messaged to say Leah's doing OK. If you're worried about today's points tally, you'll need to—"

"No, I'm just..." Jessica hesitated as Pablo nudged the camera to point at her. She wanted to back out of the alley, but she couldn't run from her problems any longer. She took a deep breath and forced herself to continue. "I actually wanted to ask if anyone knew where Leah was yesterday. She's batted her eyelashes at the police, so they're not even investigating her, but she and Cameron were in a secret relationship, and I get the feeling things weren't too rosy between them. I wonder if she might have been involved in... what happened to him."

A trickle of sweat broke free from her hairline and inched its way down her forehead then onto her cheek. She felt the eye of the camera on her. If anyone saw her now—saw her accusing the nation's favourite, doe-eyed contestant—they'd detest her. But Jessica needed to point the finger at Leah as bait.

"That's quite a theory," Pablo said, nudging the camerawoman to zoom in. "Do you really think she might have been involved in his death?"

Jessica ignored his question. "She's actually in hospital now because of that relationship." She checked Pablo, making sure he was in his usual position by the camerawoman's shoulder. "She got a tattoo to match one of his, and it became infected. Who'd have thought so much trouble could be caused by a tiny line drawing of a whisk?"

Her eyes flicked to the camerawoman's face, and she saw the horror of understanding crawl over it and grow. Then the blonde looked past Jessica to the exit of the alley. She was short and had a slim, delicate frame. But she carried a heavy piece of equipment that could be deadly.

The camerawoman started forward, and Jessica's heart slammed against her ribs. *Move*, her brain screamed, but she couldn't let the woman get away. She was a killer, and she was going to escape.

The woman barrelled towards Jessica, her legs a blur of speed, despite the enormous camera she carried. She wouldn't stop!

41

As the camerawoman pounded the final few steps to the exit of the alley, Jessica squeezed her eyes shut. She braced herself for impact, but instead of something ramming into her chest, she felt a hard yank on her shoulder. Someone pulled her clear of the alley, and as she opened her eyes, she saw a tangle of limbs, a tumbling camera, and the satisfied grin of young Officer Billy as he pinned the runner to the ground.

"I don't know what you've done," Billy said, "but anyone darting away like that is up to no good."

Pablo raced forwards, his phone held up to record what was happening. "She's the killer." He turned to Jessica. "She is, right? She had that whisk tattoo on her shoulder, and she ran away the moment you mentioned it. Was she... Did she...?"

He was even more in the dark than Jessica, who was making a leap with the little information she had. She asked Billy to take off the camerawoman's gloves. "I think you'll find another tattoo there that matches one of Cameron's. It's a wedding ring."

"She's his wife?" Pablo almost dropped his phone in surprise—but not quite.

"We were separated," the camerawoman spat, sounding as vicious as bubbling oil. "And it was barely a marriage anyway. I thought we were in love, but he was just using me. He made it seem like a whirlwind romance, but the tattoo on our fingers had barely healed when he *found out* what production company I worked for. He said I must be able to call in a favour for my new husband and get him on the baking show, even though his application had been rejected. I can't believe I fell for it."

Billy listened in open-mouthed surprise. He took the handcuffs from his belt but didn't seem to know what to do with them.

However, the camerawoman showed no sign of running again. She merely grimaced with loathing. "I turned down my job on the main crew because he said if people found out we were married, they'd think I was helping him win. But really, he just wanted to get away with cheating with any contestant who would have him. He didn't even hide it, but when the papers reported his antics, he said they were lying. He didn't know that my sister is also a camerawoman. I gave her my spot on the main crew, and she told me everything. When I confronted him, he said he didn't need me anymore. He told me to go ahead and file for divorce. I didn't think I'd ever see him again, but then he had the nerve to show up here. That was after getting my sister fired for giving him what he deserved."

For the first time in days, Jessica's thoughts felt clear—they were as smooth as mirror glaze. The loose threads in this strange case tied up in ways she could never have expected. Of course the chocoholic Meg on the regular crew was this woman's sister. That much was clear now Jessica took the time to really look at this angry woman's face. Meg must have been the one who switched Cameron's sugar and salt. And Jessica had been right to think Cameron's wife was the answer to this mystery—if only she'd known how close she was to the woman all along.

Jessica searched through the web of connections in her mind for the final few unanswered questions. "Did he know you would be here?"

A fat tear rolled down the woman's cheek. "He didn't care. When I saw him with his arm around that Leah, I ... I couldn't believe it. I could see in his eyes that he was using her, too, and then I heard him reject her and laugh in her face. She was devastated, and I realised what I had to do. He needed to be stopped."

"So you stopped him," Billy said, finally seeming to remember that he was in charge. "But that wasn't your decision to make. Don't worry, you'll have plenty of time to think over what you've done in prison."

"Wait!" Jessica called as he led the killer away. There was still one wildly waving thread that she couldn't understand how to tie back to everything. "What about the letter? Did you send it to Cameron? Did you tell him things about my family?"

The look of confusion on the camerawoman's face was unmistakeable. She appeared to have no clue what Jessica was talking about. But she had to. She was the last link in the strange chain that tied Cameron and his death to Little Quillington.

"Where did it come from? What do you know?" Jessica chased her to the police car, and she even raised her fists and banged on the door. But then Pippa crushed her in a tight hug.

She'd forgotten her friend was even there, but her presence was just what Jessica needed. Pippa was soothing butter on the red burn of her confusion. Jessica was frustrated not to get an answer about the letter, but Pippa whispered reminders that she'd caught a killer and brought them to justice.

The two women returned to Just My Type and retold the dramatic capture to Hattie, who gasped and squealed throughout. As Jessica neared the end of the tale, she got stuck again on the mystery of the letter Cameron had brought to Little Quillington. If his angry wife hadn't sent it, where had it come from?

Hattie whipped up a delicious charcuterie board somehow in the stockroom's rudimentary kitchen, and the three women talked late into the evening. Long after the shop was closed and their voices were tired and croaking, they were all still confused by the note's origins.

Jessica was grateful Cameron's killer was locked away. The target on her back had been heavier than she'd realised. Having that weight lifted felt good. But something very strange was still going on in Little Quillington. Someone knew secrets about her family, but what those were and the person's motives for keeping them were impossible to guess.

She sipped one of Hattie's incredible nutmeg lattes as she thought the matter over. Pippa wrapped an arm around Jessica's shoulders and promised that together, they'd get to the bottom of the mystery.

Epilogue

Three weeks later

The streets were once more strung with bunting as Jessica drove into Little Quillington. But this time, the fabric flapping in the warm breeze was not a brightly coloured celebration of the summer fête. This bunting was black, and it was hung in commemoration of a terrible event that Jessica still could not fully believe.

When sweet, young Leah was announced as the winner of the Great British Street Bakes Showdown, Jessica had thought she understood sadness. She'd worked so hard to win the contest—even solving the murder of a competitor along the way. But it hadn't been enough. And when Jessica returned to real life after the contest, her business struggles felt as tough as creaming butter fresh from the fridge. Resuming the hustle for pitches and the juggling of invoices and credit cards didn't feel like the adventure it had in her twenties.

But she hadn't truly known sadness then. Even during the days when people stopped more often for selfies with "the sweet-toothed sleuth," as the papers called her, than to buy her food, she hadn't known what it meant to have a heavy heart.

Now, though, she understood.

The rosemary in her window boxes swirled through the air as Jessica parked her truck. The velvet touch of the herb brought fresh tears. She was amazed her eyes had any more to shed, but they flowed as they had done for days. She might never stop crying.

Her grandma was dead.

Earlier that week, she'd ignored calls from her brother. It was odd for him to ring out of the blue, but she was too busy working to listen to a lecture about arguing with her aunt.

When Pippa rang right after him, Jessica set aside her half-whipped cream and answered. Then her friend had stayed on the phone as she wept until she was hoarse.

"Come home," Pippa had insisted.

But if Jessica came back, it would be real, so she'd pushed the plea away. For days, she'd wiped red-rimmed eyes while serving cakes and tried to lose herself in baking. Customers veered away, and Jessica didn't blame them. Food trucks provided fun treats and adventures in indulgence, and the mood was dampened by a spirit as dull as a day-old croissant.

Then her brother called once again, and her nose tingled with notes of home.

As Jessica climbed down from her food truck onto the cobbles of Little Quillington, she felt the firmness of belonging. This place was where her grandma had raised her. It was where her best friend lived. It was the source of her family's long legacy.

Little Quillington was also, she found as her long legs tripped on a loose stone and left her sprawled on the ground, a place that could still surprise her. *Like Bambi on ice*, the memory of her grandma chuckled, and Jessica smiled for the first time in days. She was about to push up from her inelegant sprawl when she spotted something moving beneath her truck. It was a tiny bundle of fur that blew towards her on a breeze.

Jessica reached out her hand, and the fluff leapt in it and clung on. Slowly, the bundle revealed a pink nose at one end and a comma-shaped tail at the other.

"I know you," Jessica murmured to the tiny kitten, staring at it in wonder.

When she'd gone to live with her grandma at ten, the woman had knitted her a cat that looked just like this, right down to the sweet little tabby's tigerlike markings. Jessica had loved it even more when she'd learned it was a replica of her grandma's own pet growing up.

"I really do know you." Jessica looked to see where the cat had come from. But there wasn't another soul on the street. The kitten nuzzled into her palm as tightly as if she'd always been there, and Jessica murmured the name her grandma's cat had once proudly borne, "Miss Marple."

This sweet companion was exactly what she needed that day. She would be facing her family shortly—attending the reading of her grandma's will on her brother's insistence. Miss Marple was small enough to fit in her generous pockets during that event, and the cute little thing would allow her to cope with a room full of people who didn't want her there.

Though, Jessica reminded herself as she headed to the square, at least one family member was on her side. Someone had thrown the paper airplane at her on the day of the head-to-head, and it contained helpful information only an Askew would know.

She didn't doubt her aunt had continued to work against her and her grandma, and Jessica had low expectations for what she might inherit. She hoped for the cute little toadstool lamp from her grandma's dressing table; it contained a chipped family of porcelain mice the two of them had exchanged stories about on stormy evenings. If she could sit in the glow of that light once again, she would always have a home.

But she wouldn't put it past Aunt Enriqueta to have taken even that.

Jessica, Pippa, Madeline, and Hattie already had plans to meet in the Quill and Well pub as soon as the proceedings were finished. She could drown her sorrows over the loss of the lamp there if needed. Miss Marple's sweet snuggles would help too. The tabby's fur was as soft as powdered sugar. Jessica stroked it as she walked across the square and onto Askew Avenue.

Little did she know that she was heartbeats away from changing her life entirely.

***

Find out what Jessica has inherited and continue your adventure in Little Quillington in the second book of The Parchment Paper Mysteries, *Lime and Punishment*[1].

---

1. https://books2read.com/LimeAndPunishment

While you make a fresh pot of tea to accompany your reading, catch up on the local news from Little Quillington with issue one of *The Quill*[3]. The village paper includes sneak peaks of local life, Askew family history, and a bonus recipe.

---

[2]. https://books2read.com/LimeAndPunishment

[3]. *https://BookHip.com/QVDANCB*

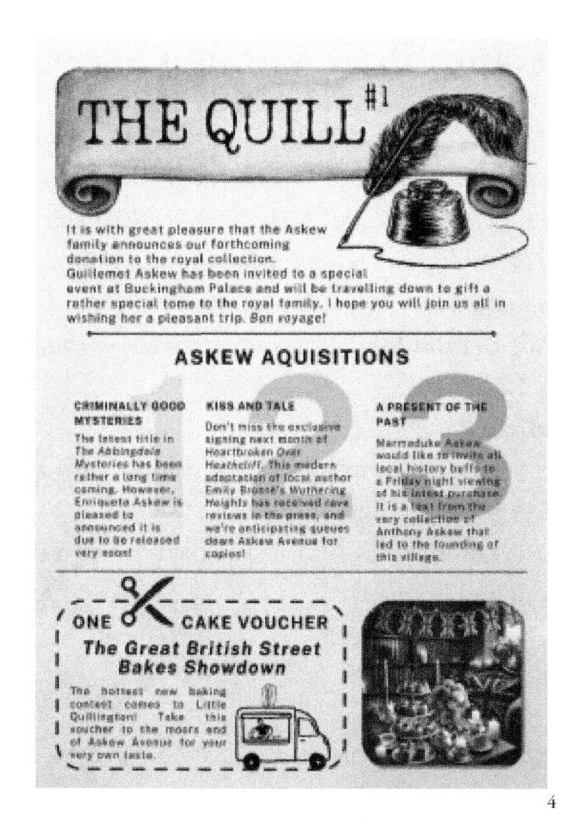

THE QUILL #1

It is with great pleasure that the Askew family announces our forthcoming donation to the royal collection. Guillemet Askew has been invited to a special event at Buckingham Palace and will be travelling down to gift a rather special tome to the royal family. I hope you will join us all in wishing her a pleasant trip. Bon voyage!

ASKEW AQUISITIONS

CRIMINALLY GOOD MYSTERIES

The latest title in The Abbingdale Mysteries has been rather a long time coming. However, Enriqueta Askew is pleased to announced it is due to be released very soon!

KISS AND TALE

Don't miss the exclusive signing next month of Heartbroken Over Heathcliff. This modern adaptation of local author Emily Brossë's Wuthering Heights has received rave reviews in the press, and we're anticipating queues down Askew Avenue for copies!

A PRESENT OF THE PAST

Marmaduke Askew would like to invite all local history buffs to a Friday night viewing of his latest purchase. It is a text from the early collection of Anthony Askew that led to the founding of this village.

ONE CAKE VOUCHER
The Great British Street Bakes Showdown

The hottest new baking contest comes to Little Quillingtan! Take this voucher to the moors end of Askew Avenue for your very own taste.

Make sure to grab the recipes mentioned in this book too...

---

4. https://BookHip.com/QVDANCB

Recipe: Prizewinning Scones

Jessica's recipe note: As I told Pippa, this recipe isn't magic, but it does create some truly delicious scones. If you're looking for a quick and easy bake that will make you feel like a fancy English lady ready for afternoon tea, this is the one to try. In the event of surprise guests, you can skip soaking the raisins / sultanas, but that step does add an extra burst of pleasure if you've got time for it.

Makes 12 scones

Ingredients:

750g / 5 cups self-raising / self-rising flour

185g / 4 ⅔ cups butter

120g / ¾ cup sultanas / raisins (soaked in hot water for at least an hour and drained)

120g / ½ cup caster sugar

350ml / 1 ½ cups milk

Method:

1. Preheat oven to 180°C / 160°C fan / 350°F.

2. Rub the butter into the flour to achieve a breadcrumb consistency.

3. Stir in the sugar and sultanas / raisins.

4. Add ¾ of the milk and stir to combine without overworking. Add enough additional milk to make a dough that just comes away from the sides. It will be pillow soft but not sticky.

5. On a floured surface, roll out to 4cm / 1.5in thick. Cut with a 7cm fluted cutter, reshaping the dough as lightly as possible.

AND THEN THERE WERE SCONES

6. Place on a lined baking tray and brush the tops with milk.

7. Bake for 15-20 minutes until golden brown.

Recipe: Yorkshire Barm Brack

Jessica's recipe note: This cake tastes far more delicious than anything without butter has a right to be. It's light and moist, and as it contains no butter itself, you can spread some of the golden good stuff on your slice to add a little luxury. Yorkshire barm brack is perfect to eat alongside a cup of tea and is a delicate alternative to a traditional fruit cake.

Ingredients:
300ml / 10fl oz boiling water
4 tea bags (ideally Yorkshire tea)
275g / 1 ¾ cups plain / all-purpose flour
2 tsp baking powder
2 tsp mixed spices*
150g / ¾ cup caster sugar
110g / ½ cup dark brown sugar
350g / 2 ⅓ cup mixed dried fruits
1 large egg (lightly beaten)
* include any of your favourites, such as cinnamon, ginger, nutmeg, cardamom, all-spice

Method:
1. Add the sugars, fruit and teabags to a bowl of boiling water. Cover with a tea towel and leave to steep overnight. The next day, remove the teabags and either discard them or pop into a fresh pot of boiling water to make a delicious hot, sweet drink.

2. Grease and line a 2lb loaf tin.

3. Preheat oven to 160°C / 140°C fan / 320°F.

4. Add the flour, baking powder and spices to a bowl. Mix together.

5. Stir in the fruit and the liquid it soaked in.

6. Finally, stir in the beaten egg then spoon the mix into the loaf tin.

7. Bake for 90 minutes or until a skewer comes out clean. Allow to cool fully in the tin before removing and cutting off a large slice to enjoy.

Author's Note

Dear Reader,

Thank you for joining me on this journey into Little Quillington and all the mysteries it contains. If you've enjoyed Jessica's adventures, head over to my website (MatildaSwift.com[1]) to **sign up for the mailing list** and learn about upcoming books in this series, enjoy free stories, grab ARC team invites, and (most importantly) see adorable photos of the real Madame Poirot and Miss Marple (they're cute enough alone to sign up for). Please also **rate and review** this book wherever you can. Reviews help other readers find the book, which is essential for the series to succeed.

Then you can head straight into the next book in the series here: *Lime and Punishment*[2]. Find out what Jessica has inherited and what it means for the future of the Rolling Pin, her friendship with Pippa, and her role in the Askew family. *Lime and Punishment*[3] is packed with twists and turns you won't want to miss.

See you again soon,
Matilda Swift

---

1. https://matildaswift.com/
2. *https://books2read.com/LimeAndPunishment*
3. *https://books2read.com/LimeAndPunishment*

About the Author

Matilda Swift lives in an English village that's just a few miles away from the fictional Little Quillington.

She's originally from nearby Manchester, and after travelling the world from Madagascar to Malaysia as well as living in Hong Kong for several years, she's back amongst the hills and rain in the place she loves best.

Follow her on Instagram[1] for more updates on writing, baking, hiking, and all the fun of life in rural England.

By Matilda Swift
The Heathervale Mysteries
Rotten to the Marrow (prequel novella)
The Slay of the Land
Dying over Spilled Milk
Fresh out of Cluck
The Scream of the Crop
A Room with a Clue
Wreathed in Mystery (short story collection)

***

The Slippery Spoon Mysteries
Take the Rough with the Smoothie (prequel novella)
From Bad to Wurst
In Deep Truffle
Butter Late than Never

***

---

1. https://www.instagram.com/matildaswiftauthor/

The Parchment Paper Mysteries
Artichoke Heart of Darkness (prequel novella)
And Then There Were Scones
Lime and Punishment
For Whom the Bell Pepper Tolls
The Catcher in the Pie
matildaswift.com[2]

---

2. https://matildaswift.com/

Printed in Dunstable, United Kingdom